Items should be returned on or before the last date shown below. Items not already requested by other borrowers may be renewed in person, in writing or by telephone. To renew, please quote the number on the barcode label. To renew online a PIN is required. This can be requested at your local library.
Renew online @ **www.dublincitypubliclibraries.ie**
Fines charged for overdue items will ~~~~~~ postage incurred in rec~~~~~~~~~~~~~~~~~ ms will be charged to t~~~~~~~

Leabharlanna ~~~~~~~~~~~~~~~~ **na Cliath**
Dul ~~~~~~~~~~~~~~~~~~~~

Date Due	Date Due	Date Due

The Angry Land

He pays his debts with hot lead!

This is the story of a kid who turns killer, a boy who grows to manhood long before his time. Seeing no justice in the land, he takes the law into his own lightning swift hands.

The legend that grows around Billy Bascom is born the day they planted the cross that read: 'Here lie Ben Ober and Jim Boone; hanged for cattle rustling May 14, 1880.'

There should have been a third name on that board: that of Billy Bascom. But the kid had been rescued from Jason Ryan's lynch party just in time. The thirst to avenge the death of his friends, and the murder of his saviour, has changed Billy into New Mexico's most ruthless gunslinger.

And no man is going to be his undoing.

The Angry Land

Samuel A. Peeples

A Black Horse Western
ROBERT HALE

© The Estate of Samuel A. Peeples 2016
First published in Great Britain 2016

ISBN 978-0-7198-1999-5

The Crowood Press
The Stable Block
Crowood Lane
Ramsbury
Marlborough
Wiltshire SN8 2HR

www.crowood.com

Robert Hale is an imprint
of The Crowood Press

The right of Samuel A. Peeples to be identified as
author of this work has been asserted by his Estate
in accordance with the Copyright, Designs
and Patents Act 1988

Printed and bound in Great Britain by
CPI Antony Rowe, Chippenham and Eastbourne

EDITOR'S NOTES

It's no secret that I am a long time fan of Samuel A. Peeples, who I first 'met' as a very young girl in his persona as Brad Ward, an author for ACE westerns.

I wrote my one and only fan letter ever to 'Mr Ward' after reading one of his westerns I had inherited from my much older brother, Leonard, after he enlisted in the US Army. 'Inherited' probably is the wrong word: being a precocious reader, I actually pilfered his vast collection; and read every single book.

Sam brought the west alive. Unlike Clarence Mulford and Zane Grey, Sam's writing was very contemporary. No exaggerated dialect or archaic slang; just beautiful prose describing not only the land, but vividly portraying even the most minor characters. And the dialogue: I don't think anyone, even today, comes close to creating the kind of believable dialogue that flows from the mouths of the characters and makes them distinct and incredibly real.

I had long forgotten the fan letter once it was mailed, but – months later – I actually received a one-page reply written in much the same manner as the way he wrote his stories. Short, sweet and right to the point. The one thing he told me that has stayed with me forever is – after I had told him I was a girl and I wanted to write cowboy stories (yes, I was that young) – was that women could do anything a man could do, even write westerns; and sometimes even better.

That was enough to inspire me to write. And if you look closely at my writing, you will see a lot of Sam's influence. It is my hope more people will now be able to enjoy Sam's original works with a fresh set of eyes, and a new sense of appreciation.

Kit Prate

AUTHOR'S NOTE

The Angry Land is based upon the most famous of all southwestern legends. While the value of historical fact is known and respected by the author, there is very little about the brutal, tangled facts that has not been told and retold. The legend is another matter. It has persisted for a hundred years, often changed in detail but never in clarity of outline. Like most legends, it deals with good and evil, and the bad man who did some good, and contains a great deal of historical truth since it reflects the mood of a time and place long gone. It seemed worthwhile to this writer to subjugate the letter of fact to the spirit of legend in this novel, but it is only fair to point out the major liberties that were taken. Governor Winston Carlisle never existed, nor is his character that of any actual Territorial Governor; however, to demonstrate his activities are not beyond belief, one of his real-life counterparts once sold the irreplaceable archives of the *palacio* by the pound to local merchants to be used as wrapping paper. Conchita Noriega is entirely fictional, and had no real counterpart. The fiesta in Santa Fe is in September, not in mid-year as implied in the story, nor was the wonderful old structure so burned. Liberties have been taken with dates, chronology and distances, and although certain historical characters can be easily identified despite their fictional names, characterizations at variance with historical fact are nonetheless true to the spirit of the legend in which white is always white and black is always black. In final apology, while this may not be the way it really happened, it is the way it will be remembered.

7

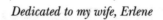
Dedicated to my wife, Erlene

PROLOGUE

New Mexico, 1880

The brassy sun stood an hour past the summit of the cloudless sky, and heat pressed mercilessly against the dry land. The rolling benchland below the sun-whitened hills was dotted with yucca white with powder-fine sand, their shadows dark puddles about their bases. A sullen, brooding place that fought against encroachment; the steel-clad conquerors from the South had felt the resentment of this land; the naked savages who had once dwelt here had respected its bitter strength; now it was the Americanos' turn to feel its fury. The tall men who brought great herds of half-wild cattle, seeking to build here their private empires, were stronger than any who had come before them, but in their selfishness, under the brutal lash of heat and dryness and the hatred of the land itself, they quarrelled and fought. A dust whorl danced along the ground, coating the bleached clumps of soapweed and mesquite and creosote bush. A rattler, coiled in the shade of an outcropping of rock, buzzed its electric warning. An empty, aching loneliness lay across the silent hills. This was the angry land.

Below the shoulder of the hills began the flat valley, covered with grama, galeta and buffalo grass, which brought the cattle herds here. A dry creek bed ran southward and on the far side rose the green cloud of a Rio Grande cottonwood. It stood alone, unfaltering in its lonely vigil, a single green defiance of the harsh land. Beneath the tree, in the meagre shade, stood five men, and a sixth, no more than a boy, squatted on his haunches, his hands tied behind his back, his eyes lifted to a thick branch overhead. Two men were hung there, one dead and still, slowly pivoting at the end of the rope that encircled his neck, the other fighting death, his body arching, his legs kicking wildly in a final, grim dance. These were the violent men.

CHAPTER 1

Billy Bascom squinted against the glare of the sun and considered the jerking figure of Ben Ober thoughtfully. Ober was dying hard, and Ryan and his men were enjoying it. Billy's full-lipped, mobile mouth curved down slightly at the corners. He had an itch under his arms, but, with his hands tied behind him with a rawhide thong, he could do nothing about it. Funny, he was going to be dancing like poor Ben in a minute, and the most important thing to him was an itch. Billy's ever-present smile peeled away his lips from his prominent, white upper teeth, and he looked even younger than his nineteen years.

Bob Oringer loomed over him, and Billy shifted his gaze to the Triangle ramrod. Oringer was a big man, but not fat. Grim amusement crinkled the corners of his pale blue eyes; Oringer laughed hardest at the most unpleasant things.

'Enjoyin' the show, kid?' Oringer asked. 'That's why I saved you until last. Figured you'd like to see your pards swing. They'll be waiting in hell for you.'

'Just like I'll be waiting for you, Bob,' Billy answered, still smiling.

For a moment their eyes held level, and then the bigger man swung the flat of his hand in a brutal blow that dumped the boy sideways to the sand. It coated his sweat-wet skin and itched unbearably, but Billy's smile remained fixed to his lips.

'Someday I'm going to blow you apart, Bob. I'm going to scatter the filth you're made of.'

For an instant Oringer balanced there, then he laughed aloud. 'Sure you are! Just like you're getting' away this time!' He sobered, bent down. 'You've got about five minutes to live, you stinkin' little bastard!'

'Leave him alone, Bob,' a tall, heavily built man said, coming up to them. 'You know any prayers, Billy, you better start saying them.'

Billy rolled, forced himself back to a sitting position. He spat dirt from his mouth. The side of his face, where Oringer's blow had caught him, was livid, and a small cut oozed blood. 'I'll leave prayin' to sanctimonious bastards like you, Ryan,' he said, viciously.

Oringer started forward again, arm raised for a chopping blow, but Ryan stopped him. Jason Ryan was past fifty and had spent his life in the sun. His long-seamed skin had darkened to the colour of wet wood. 'I said to leave him alone,' he ordered. He raised his head to look up at the two hanged men. His eyes were expressionless. 'Jerry, bring up his horse. Let's get this done.'

Oringer's grin broadened, and he bent, gripped Bascom's tied hands and lifted savagely. A grimace of pain shot across the boy's face as he was jerked to his feet.

Another Triangle rider led up a sorrel mare. The horse rolled its eyes and shied from being brought close to the two hanged men, and the man controlled the animal by brute strength, sawing on the reins.

Oringer swung Bascom roughly around, then boosted him into the saddle. 'I'll give Conchita your love, kid,' he said and laughed again.

'Do that,' Billy Bascom answered, and leaned forward to spit directly into Oringer's face.

The Triangle foreman cursed and swung a vicious blow at the younger man's face, but Billy dodged back in the saddle, and the blow missed and spun Oringer half around. Ryan's sharp voice stopped him when he turned back.

'Get it done!'

Oringer held still, breathing hard, his eyes narrowed as he wiped spittle from his cheek. 'I'll remember this when I'm layin' with your greaser girl, kid. I'll remember it an' do my laughin' then.' He spun about. 'All right, Jerry, get the rope over the branch.'

Billy Bascom sat at ease in the saddle, his face composed. It wouldn't be long now, he thought, and wondered at the simple fact that he was not afraid. He remembered how Ben Uber had cursed and raved, and how Jim Boone had cried and begged. Boone had been the first hanged. He had died quickly, without much fuss, when his horse had been driven from under him. Not like Ober, who had fought death with all his strength. Billy eyed Uber's slowly stiffening figure; there was only the slightest quiver of the legs now.

It was still and hot. The heat pressed in upon him with tangible force. Billy looked out across the browned valley, his grey eyes narrowed against the glare. I should be afraid, he thought, but I'm not. Why? It isn't because I don't enjoy living. He closed his eyes. There were many things he liked, the sharp bite of tequila, the sweetness of a girl's mouth half-opened against his own.... But he had little thought for the things he had known; it was the new things, the things he had never had time to try, that he regretted. It was only a vague regret, like passing up the shiny pair of boots in Dolan's General Store for the lack of hard money, or making do with beans and bacon when there was nothing better. Keenest of all was a slow stiffing of resentment that he could not even things with Oringer, yes, and with Jason Ryan, too. Billy opened his eyes and stared down at the two men.

The man, Jerry, tossed a rope upward, but it fell short. He cursed, bent to retrieve it, coiled it and threw again. It went up and over the limb of the tree. Billy began to hum a tune.

> 'Can she bake a cherry pie, Billy Boy, Billy Boy?
> Can she bake a cherry pie, charmin' Billy?'

The remaining two Triangle men stood to one side. Rank Ballew was pale and kept staring up at the two dead men. Paul Dorman was grinning, enjoying the show. Ballew was going to be sick, Billy thought. Then Jerry dropped the noose over his head and clinched it tight against his throat, the hard knot just under his left ear. This is it, Billy thought, without excitement and without fear. This is it....

13

Bob Oringer walked to the rear of Bascom's horse. He licked his lips, and his smile went crooked. Jason Ryan looked coldly up into Billy's face, and then turned his attention toward a distant yucca, a tall, thin candle of God. Jerry stared up into Billy's face with an obscene expectancy. The other two men watched expressionlessly.

Five men like these are going to watch me die, Billy thought. The dirty bastards! I'd like to piss on them, like a dog against a tree. I'd like to show them how small they really are....

Oringer held still, savouring the moment, fixing the scene in his mind, like a boy trying to remember every detail of some special event. And he waited too long. Hoofs cracked sharply, and three horsemen veered down the slope, spilling dust into the air as they drew up. Billy heard Oringer's 'What the hell?'

Then a new voice cut in. 'Havin' a party, Jason?'

Billy saw Ryan withdraw his gaze from the distant yucca and turn to face the three newcomers. The man in the lead sat at ease, his hat pushed back from his forehead. He was tall and lean of build, with a young-old face that had humour and hardness in equal mixture. His mouth was a straight line, and there was an ungiving jut to his chin. He held a Winchester across his lap, and the muzzle, as if by chance, was in line with Ryan's body.

The Triangle owner's hard-rock features didn't change. He met the other's eyes arrogantly. 'Mind your own business, Burnett.'

A second man urged his horse close to the tall man. Billy felt a mild surprise at his appearance. He wore whipcord britches, high, narrow-legged boots, a white shirt with a black tie, and a corduroy jacket with elbow patches of yellow leather. When he spoke, his voice was soft, with an odd, rising intonation that caught Billy's attention.

'My God, Ryan, are you out of your mind? You've killed two men – are you going to hang another?'

'That I am,' Ryan answered, slowly. The hard, cold assurance of the man did not change. 'Oringer, get on with it.'

'Tell him to wait, Ryan,' the tall rider cut in, quickly. The muzzle of the rifle shifted slightly.

'I told you to mind your own business, Burnett,' Ryan said,

softly. None of the Triangle men moved.

'I make up my own mind what is my business,' Burnett returned. 'You're on Horn land, Ryan. If there's any hanging done, we'll do it.'

Oringer moved angrily. 'Goddamn, now look here ...'

Burnett's long face twisted. Anger showed for the first time. 'Don't say anything, Bob,' he interrupted, savagely. 'The way it stands I'm minded to cut the kid loose and give him a gun. Maybe I will yet. You speak up again, and I give you my promise, I will.'

Oringer held still. His face twisted with anger, but he said nothing.

The man in the corduroy jacket urged his horse closer to Ryan. 'What have these men done, Ryan?'

The Triangle owner's insolent eyes stared at the rifle muzzle for an instant, then moved to the other man. 'It's our affair.'

'I'm making it mine,' the slender man said.

He must be English, Billy thought. His reddish face looked soft, and his voice had a high edge to it, but inside, it was Billy's guess, he was as hard as Burnett.

'I want no trouble with Horn, Trumbull,' Ryan said, slowly. His arrogance was held in abeyance, but not gone. 'This is Triangle business. Billy Bascom and his two pards, Ben Ober and Jim Boone, have been stealing me blind. We've lost eighty head of cows this last month. We cut Bascom's trail, and followed them here. That's it.'

Trumbull frowned. 'You mean you take the law into your own hands?'

'You're new out here.' Ryan said it almost as if it were an insult. 'You don't understand. You catch a rustler – you hang him.'

Burnett shook his head. 'You hang him if you catch him in the act – and on your own property. You don't hang a man – even a rustler – on somebody else's land.'

'I hang them where I catch them,' Ryan snapped. His temper ate like a canker into his self-control. He looked at Oringer, at the rest of his men and then at Burnett and the rifle.

He's trying to decide if Burnett's bluffing, Billy thought. If he knew him as well as I do, he'd know Burnett never bluffed in his

15

life. Aloud he said, 'How about that, Pete? Goin' to watch the show? You've still got time to watch the third act.'

Burnett didn't look at him. The humour had drained from his face, leaving only hard rock. 'The show's over, Billy,' he said. 'Jake, ride over and cut the kid's hands free, then give him your gun.'

Ryan opened his mouth as if he wanted to say something, then closed it. His eyes were narrowed. They remained fixed to the muzzle of the rifle. His body was held rigid, controlled as firmly as his anger. Deliberately, almost scornfully, he raised his eyes to look once more at the distant yucca.

The third rider moved against Billy's mare, and a knife glistened, then cut the rawhide thongs that bound his hands. Billy drew his hands in front of him, began to chafe them together. He forced his numbed fingers to work, rubbing his wrists. Slowly, agonizingly, feeling returned to them. His crooked grin peeled away his lips from his white teeth. He held out his hand, and the man named Jake placed a heavy Colt revolver in it. Instantly Billy ducked out of the noose as Jake loosened it, and spurred the mare. She bounded forward, then wheeled to the urging of his knee.

'You got ten seconds, Oringer!' Billy Bascom yelled. 'Fight or run!' He held the Colt casually in his left hand, across the saddle horn. He began to hum again.

Oringer stopped smiling. He licked at his lips. He looked toward Ryan, but the Triangle owner was looking past him. Oringer turned his eyes on the others, taking his time turning back to face the boy he had intended to hang. For one long instant he held there, then jerked to one side, his right hand flashing to his holstered gun.

Billy Bascom's shot sounded even as Oringer started to move. Oringer staggered to the impact of lead and went down, his gun flying into the sun-bleached sand. He started to groan and curse. His right leg was twisted beneath him, and blood began to stain his woollen britches.

The sorrel mare had not shied at the gunshot, and Billy sat the saddle almost casually. He held the Colt level before him. His half-smile didn't change. His hummed tune was audible as he squinted down the barrel of the gun. The muzzle was steady. The boy's thumb drew back the hammer. Oringer stopped cursing, and his eyes bulged. His lips began to move, but no sound came out.

Then Trumbull's quiet voice asked, 'Are you going to kill him the same dirty way he was going to kill you?'

For one brief instant the boy held there, the faint smile on his lips, his soft voice humming his song. Then the humming stopped. The muzzle of the Colt lowered an inch and Bascom looked at Trumbull. He looked for a weakness in the other's eyes, and found none, only a patient sorrow for the violence of men. Without looking toward Oringer, he said, 'You're unlucky, Bob. You're going to have time to think about the next time I see you.'

His smile widened, and he raised his head to look toward Jason Ryan. 'Don't push your luck, Ryan. You're a big man. A lot bigger than me. You throw a longer shadow than I ever will. But you trouble me again, an' I'll remember what you done to Ben an' Jim, an' I'll kill you. Maybe I will anyway. I don't never know exactly what I'm fixin' to do next. Now ride out.'

Ryan's gaze was withdrawn slowly from the distance. His face was unreadable. He looked at Trumbull, ignoring Billy Bascom. 'You'll regret this,' he said, flatly. 'You will regret it a long time.' For an instant he sat still, then turned away. 'Jerry, get Oringer on his horse.'

The cursing Bob Oringer was helped into a saddle after a neckerchief had been knotted about his leg to stop the bleeding. His face was pale, and his eyes were closed. He swayed in the saddle as the Triangle men rode off.

Pete Burnett stared after them, then raised his head to look at the two dead men. 'Jake, cut them down an' bring them in. We'll bury them on the hill back of the big house.'

Trumbull looked once at the hanged men, then shuddered. '"The land of sudden justice,"' he murmured, half to himself. Then he turned to face Billy Bascom. The youth was still smiling, holding Jake's Colt in his hand.

Pete Burnett bent to restore the rifle to the saddle boot, then looked quizzically at the boy. The hardness had been replaced with the softening touch of humour. 'You losin' your touch, Billy?' he asked. 'That was poor shootin'. Or you developin' a mean streak?'

'Maybe I wanted it to hurt,' he said. His sudden laughter rang out. 'Don't take none to the feel of a rope about my neck. Ever happen to you, Pete?'

Burnett smiled and shook his head. 'Close a couple times.' He frowned after the dust-raising figures of the Triangle riders. 'You three drunk, lettin' Ryan come up on you?'

'Tired,' Billy said. 'Up all three nights hand runnin'. Stealin' cows ain't all fun.' His light-hued eyes went to Trumbull's face and read the sudden surprise there. He watched Trumbull carefully. 'I stole some Triangle stock, same as I cut out a head or two of Horn. But Ryan didn't catch me at it.'

Trumbull frowned uncertainly. 'You're telling me you stole some of my cattle? I don't believe I understand.' He looked at Pete Burnett.

The Horn foreman rubbed one lean hand along his jaw. 'Billy's speakin' plain,' he said. 'Things are done certain ways – you hang a man when you catch him stealin' your cows, not when you just think he's stolen some. Maybe the difference ain't too clear, but it's there.'

Trumbull stared for an instant, then smiled. His round face was red from exposure to the sun, and he touched his prominent nose gingerly. It was badly sunburned and would peel soon.

'It makes as much sense as most things out here, Pete,' he agreed. His glance returned to Billy. 'My name is Harry Trumbull. I own the Horn ranch. You seem to know Pete, my foreman.'

'Old friends,' Billy answered. 'Pete half-raised me.' He winked at Burnett, then sobered. 'You didn't save much when you saved me from hangin', Mr Trumbull – but such as I am, I'm grateful.' He frowned up at the branch of the tree. 'Reckon I'm out of business on my own. Horn happen to need a good hand?'

For a moment Trumbull didn't understand. He was aware of Burnett's quick glance, and even Jake looked at them. For some reason beyond Trumbull's ken, the moment had become tense. The sense of the ridiculous that had so often assailed him worked now, and he smiled.

'Are you asking me for a job, Billy?'

The youth nodded. He was smiling, but his pale eyes were cold. 'I'm askin'.'

Trumbull's first impulse was to laugh, but he held it back. The boy was a self-confessed, almost-hanged cattle thief; and yet there was no doubt of his seriousness. There were many things here in the American West that Harry Trumbull had found beyond his comprehension, but one thing he had learned: never to take anything for granted nor on surface appearance.

'You rode with Pete?' Trumbull asked. Bascom nodded. His face was as smooth as a girl's and his indolent half-smile held something disturbing behind it, as if he expected Trumbull to refuse him the job. Trumbull looked at Burnett. The foreman's face was blank of expression, but Trumbull sensed in that instant that Burnett's silence spoke in favour of the boy. Abruptly the Englishman nodded. 'All right, Billy,' he said. 'We can always use another good man.'

Burnett came up then. His face reflected neither approval nor disapproval. He nodded at Billy. 'That your bedroll over under the tree? Get it, then help Jake with the job. The two of you can take care burying them. Come up to the house when you're ready. I'll say the words.'

Bascom's sudden grin was warm. The coldness of his colourless eyes seemed to thaw, leaving him no more than the boy he seemed. He danced the mare about, and his light, carefree voice called out, 'Here's your repeater, Jake. It throws low and to the left. Remind me to fix the sights for you.'

Trumbull sat still, not sure he had done the right thing. Burnett puzzled him most of the time. The Westerner's phlegmatic response to most queries was often disturbing. The Englishman frowned and turned his horse. Be damned if he'd ask Burnett outright! If he'd made a mistake hiring Billy Bascom, then that's the way it was. A stubborn set marked Trumbull's chin.

Burnett's horse edged closer to Trumbull's as if by accident as they rode away from the cottonwood. Burnett said, quietly, 'Billy Bascom's the best rider and the best shot in New Mexico.' Then, almost as an afterthought: 'He's killed fourteen men.'

Trumbull stiffened with shock. He saw Burnett's blue eyes watching him. The Horn ramrod was amused. Then Burnett rode on ahead, and Trumbull, after a quick, troubled look back at the youth he had saved from hanging, followed him.

CHAPTER 2

Billy Bascom watched as Jake Haley and Vaughn Morgan lowered the second pine box into a grave. Billy was leaning his weight on the shovel thrust into the pile of loose sand, and he felt tired and oddly withdrawn. It had been, he thought soberly, one hell of a day. This morning he and Ben and Jim had been planning the fun they were going to have in Lanyard that night; now Ben and Jim were dead, and Billy would never have a closer call. He supposed he should be feeling something about it, something big and important, but he didn't; he'd still like to go into Lanyard and get drunk and see Conchita....

Pete Burnett walked up to the edge of the grave and looked down. He held a worn leather-bound Bible in one hand. He cleared his throat and looked up at the sky. 'God, there isn't much anybody can say for these two gents we've just buried. They made mistakes same as the rest of us. If You've got any mercy in Your heart for the likes of them, I reckon they'll appreciate it. Amen.'

The foreman stepped back, looked at Billy. Bascom winked at him. He said, softly, 'So long, pards – see you both in hell!' Then he pulled free the shovel and bent to the task of replacing the dirt and sand. The first few shovelfuls rattled hollowly on the pine boxes. Damn, Billy thought, it must sound like thunder if you was layin' inside!

Billy shovelled steadily, and Jake did his share. They patted the mound of dirt, and Burnett drove into the ground a wooden marker on which had been burned:

20

Here lie
Ben Ober
Jim Boone
Hanged for Cattle Rustling
May 14, 1880

'Lucky your name ain't on that plank, Billy,' Burnett said.

Billy nodded, half smiling. 'Funny thing, though. It ain't taught me a damned thing. I don't feel no different. I don't even hate Ryan any more than I did before. You figger maybe I'm a little loco?'

Burnett frowned for a moment, then lifted his shoulders in a shrug. '*¿Quién sabe?* Sometimes I think the whole damned world's a little touched. But it ain't my business to say.' He frowned again. 'Ain't seen you in a year now, Billy.'

'Been west. Arizona.'

'I've heard.'

'Have you, Pete?' The smile changed to a wide grin. 'Word gets around.'

'It does that,' Burnett agreed. He looked down the slope toward the valley floor. Just off the shoulder of this low-lying hill stood the adobe walls of the Horn ranch house.

Jake Haley came around the grave, mopping his face with a red bandana. Vaughn Morgan stood silently behind him.

'Good to see you again, Billy Boy,' Haley said.

'Likewise, Jake. You, too, Morgan.'

Vaughn Morgan nodded. He was tall and rawboned, his face seamed and wrinkled, and his hands were thick with calluses. 'Hear you're stayin' on Horn,' he said. His voice was flat-toned.

Billy straightened. 'Set well with you, Morgan?'

The taller man shrugged. 'Well as anything else around a place run by a foreigner.' He walked away, down the slope toward the whitewashed adobe bunkhouse.

Billy watched him go. 'Who ruffled his hide?'

Jake Haley spat to the ground. 'Horn's havin' trouble with Ryan's Triangle. Vaughn's got cold feet.'

'Maybe I ain't been listenin' hard enough, Pete,' Billy said,

21

slowly. 'Triangle has been top dog in Lanyard County ever since Ryan drove in the first herd. Nothing I've seen has changed that.'

'Some men are hard to convince, Billy,' Pete Burnett answered, thoughtfully. 'Trumbull's one. He don't scare worth a damn. Ryan figgers he was here first. That buys him nothin' with the Englishman. As for Morgan, he says somebody threw lead at him on the north ridge two weeks ago. He says thirty a month an' found ain't ample for bein' a target.'

Billy Bascom looked after Morgan's ambling figure, then frowned. 'Figger he's talkin' straight, Pete?'

'Could be. You gun-shy all of a sudden, Billy?'

'Nope. Just rope-shy.' He laughed then, the quick effortless laughter of a boy. He sobered after a moment, though, and his pale eyes narrowed. 'Somebody shoots at me – I shoot back. That goes whether I'm ridin' for Horn or on my own.'

Pete Burnett met his gaze evenly. 'I'd be surprised if you didn't, kid,' he replied. 'Now I got one. Trumbull's green. He don't know down from up. But he's square.'

Billy didn't smile. 'It figgers. You're workin' for him, Pete.' He lifted the shovel to his shoulder and moved away. After a moment Burnett followed him. They walked in silence down the slope. Bascom left the shovel on the rack inside the stable door. Burnett finished rolling a brown-paper cigarette and tossed the bag of Bull Durham toward the youth. Billy caught it with a quick movement of his left hand. He deftly poured tobacco into a creased paper, rolled it between the fingers of his left hand with a single, quick movement.

Burnett lit his cigarette, then held the burning match for the boy to light his. He dropped the match and stepped on it. Burnett's eyes were steady. 'Why'd you hit Trumbull up for a job?'

Billy hesitated. 'I'll tell you, Pete, if you'll tell me why he hired me?'

Burnett shrugged. 'Trumbull doesn't know much, an' under-stands less. But he ain't stupid. He knows he's caught trouble. He doesn't know how much yet. Ryan hasn't pushed him hard yet, but he will. I think Trumbull senses that. Maybe he hired you because he figgered you'd kill Ryan sooner or later.'

Billy frowned. 'I can't buy that.'

'Why not, kid?' Burnett waited.

'He ain't that kind.'

Burnett drew smoke into his lungs. 'You're right. Kind he is, though, is always draggin' in some hurt critter. We got seven dogs around this layout. He found a lamb chewed by a coyote, carried it in. It's always followin' him around like he was its ma. Always fetchin' in a stray.'

'Like me,' Billy said, slowly. 'Fair enough. My turn. Maybe I figger it's a chance to stick around an' pick off Ryan an' Oringer, an' eat regular while I'm waitin'. Maybe I'm tired of things I been doin' an' want to try a new slant. Maybe I figger I'm a stray that needs some bringin' up.' He laughed, humourlessly. 'An' maybe somebody ought to tell Trumbull nobody ain't ever managed to change a lobo wolf into a house dog.'

Burnett's eyes were level. 'Maybe nobody but Trumbull ever felt it was worth the bother, kid,' he said. 'One thing more. Stay out of trouble. Let it walk on your toes 'til it hurts.'

Billy grinned. He was humming under his breath as he walked toward the bunkhouse where he had left his bedroll. After a moment, Burnett followed him. When he reached the shady side of the bunkhouse, Billy, stripped to the waist, was busily scrubbing his upper body. He was thinly built, but surprisingly heavily muscled. His back was straight, and his shoulders were wide enough to be impressive. He had removed his cartridge belt and pistol from his bedroll and they lay on the sun-bleached wooden bench. Pete frowned, and Billy grinned at him over the dirty towel he was using to dry himself.

'Seems like old times, Pete.'

'While it lasts, Billy,' Pete said. There was a grimness to his tone.

'You think it won't?'

Burnett shook his head. 'No bet's a sure thing. Trumbull deserves a fair chance. You owe him a turn, so don't start it for him. It will come soon enough.'

'That's what I like about you, Pete, always so damned optimistic.'

Billy finished mopping his upper body, tossed the towel to the bench and shook out his rumpled shirt. Dust flew. He pulled it on. 'Me, I take it as it comes. Only grown-ups worry. You never see a kid worryin' about tomorrow. I figger only damn fools ever grow up.'

'Maybe you're right, kid,' Pete replied. 'Trouble is, some of us can't help it.'

Burnett turned and walked away. He rounded the corner of the bunkhouse, and Billy watched him, a thoughtful pucker between his eyes. Then he shrugged, thrust the tails of his shirt into his pants. He buckled on his gun belt. The holster was over his left hip, a right-hand holster that placed the gun butt forward. To draw the weapon the boy's left hand had to bend inward and reverse the revolver as it was drawn. But for Billy, being ambidextrous, it made a cross-draw possible from any angle; standing, sitting, riding, bending, falling. When the time came for gun talk, it gave him an edge; and to Billy's practical turn of mind in such matters, it was a form of life insurance that had already paid dividends. Too many times, he thought, grimly. His frown grew deeper. He looked once more toward the corner around which Burnett had gone. 'Don't start it for him....' For a moment, he held there, then slowly he unbuckled the gun belt. He held it up and looked at it for an instant, then grinned and replaced it in his bedroll. He was humming when he carried it into the cool interior of the bunkhouse.

The smell struck him first: the smell of leather, tobacco, dust, and hard-working, hard-swearing men. A long table ran down the centre of the room, and a belly stove stood at the far end. Billy walked down the room until he came to an empty bunk, and tossed his bedroll upon it. A man lying on a bunk across the room looked up at him, and Billy winked.

He made the bed, stored his belongings under it, then sat down. He pulled his boots off and lay back on the bunk. The man across the room asked, 'Want the makin's, kid?'

'I could use a smoke,' Billy answered.

The man tossed him a bag of tobacco. 'Keep it,' he said. 'I'll be bummin' smokes off'n you soon enough. The name's Oscar Wiggin.'

'Thanks, Oscar. I'm Billy Bascom.'

'I heard. Morgan's got a big mouth an' he uses it.' Wiggin grinned. 'I ain't doin' so bad myself. Forget I said it.'

Billy built a cigarette with the same quick roll of his left hand. He tucked the bag of tobacco into a shirt pocket, leaned back on the bunk.

Wiggin chuckled to himself. 'Funny thing, Billy. You hirin' on today, I mean. I'd've bet ten bucks Trumbull wasn't the kind to hire a man like you.'

Billy frowned. 'A man like me?'

Oscar nodded. His face was too fat for his bone-thin body, and his jowls quivered when he spoke. 'You're a gun, kid – loaded and pointed.'

Billy closed his eyes and sighed. 'You can make me mad if you work at it, Oscar.'

The other grinned. 'Suppose I could. No offence meant. Wasn't you I was thinkin' about.'

Billy's eyes opened. 'That make good sense to you?'

Oscar frowned. His absurdly round face was clown-like when he was serious. 'In a way. I was thinkin' of Trumbull – an' Ryan. The King of Lanyard County has tender toes, an' Trumbull steps hard without knowin' it. I'd hate to dig his grave.' Wiggin chuckled again. 'I'd like to see Ryan's face when he's told the know-nothin' Englishman's hired Billy Boy Bascom.'

Billy reached over and stubbed out his cigarette in the can bottom that served as an ashtray. Silence fell between them. Billy folded his arms behind his head and stared thoughtfully up at the smoke-streaked whitewashed ceiling. In repose his lips were slightly parted by the prominence of his upper teeth. After a while he heard Wiggin grunt and get up. Boots thudded as the other made his way outside. Through the adobe walls voices drifted. A man laughed. Water splashed in the pans on the wash bench. Rough good humour marked the voices. It made a warm feeling inside Billy Bascom. He liked the feeling of belonging, of being nailed down to one place. It had been a long time since he had tied onto an outfit. Too long, he thought soberly, then frowned.

25

The bunkhouse grew shadowy. The careless talk quieted; the Horn riders were squatting around outside, smoking, thinking their own thoughts. In a few days, Billy thought, he would fit in, become an accepted part of their lives, as they would become a part of his. It was like that with a good outfit, and Billy sensed that Trumbull would run that kind of spread. The supper triangle chimed as the cook beat upon it, and feet thudded as men moved toward the far end of the long, adobe building where the kitchen and dining hall were located. Billy sighed and sat up, bending over to pull on his boots. He stood up, stretched, then made his way outside. Some of the heat of the day still held, but there was a soft breeze from the west. It would get cooler. He made his way through the gathering dusk toward the yellow-lighted windows at the far end of the building. He heard the tinny clatter of dishes, the subdued murmur of voices. He went inside. Wiggin was sitting at the near end of the long table, and he grinned and pointed at an empty place beside him. Billy straddled the wooden bench, nodded to two or three men who looked at him. A Mexican cook came up and scooped mashed potatoes onto his plate, poured coffee. Wiggin pulled a platter of fried steak toward him and Billy helped himself.

The men ate in the silence of hungry appetites. When plates were pushed back, the Mexican came down the line, refilling cups. The man across the table said, 'I'm Hank Lewis, straw boss. We'll work your tail off, Bascom, but we'll keep you well fed an' pay you in hard money when it's due.'

Billy grinned. 'Thanks.'

Lewis was a long-faced man with drooping, yellow moustache. His eyes were a faded blue and there were deep hen tracks about them. He shovelled a chunk of apple pie into his mouth, chomped methodically. 'You'll meet the rest of the crew as we go along.' He finished the pie, drained his coffee cup, and then stood up. 'I'm beat. Turnin' in early. We're stringin' fence along the north ridge, an' five-thirty rolls around too damn soon.'

Wiggin groaned. 'You can say that twice. My gawd, Hank, my tailbone's bent from stretchin' wire. I'm goin' to be wearin' a hump

26

like a turtle, you keep me at it.'

'On you it would look good,' Hank replied, and a laugh went up.

Several of the other men spoke to Billy, and he replied to each. He was aware of the reserve toward him, but knew it would wear thin in time. He would be accepted as one of them as he always was. Just as trouble always followed. But maybe this time ... he broke off the thought. He finished his coffee, got up and went outside. Wiggin followed him.

'For a boot-black cowman's spread, Horn ain't bad,' Wiggin observed.

'I think it'll suit me,' Billy answered. 'See you around, Oscar.' He walked back toward the bunkhouse, and when Oscar followed, veered away toward the corral and stables. In the warm darkness there, he leaned against the rails and built a cigarette. He smoked thoughtfully, studying the pattern of the lights across the front of the big house up the slope, and then with sudden decision walked that way. He reached the wide veranda that sprawled across the belly of the adobe building, dropped the cigarette to the ground and stepped on it. He hesitated for an instant, then stepped up to the porch and walked toward the glass-fronted door. He stopped suddenly when a man's voice called to him from the darkness to one side.

'Looking for me, Billy?' It was Trumbull. The Englishman was seated in a wicker chair that squeaked as he shifted his weight.

Billy moved toward him. 'Yes, Mr Trumbull,' he answered. He could make out the Englishman's face from the light that filtered onto the covered porch from an open window. 'I reckon you made a mistake takin' me on.'

'It wouldn't be my first one, Billy,' Trumbull said, quietly. 'But what makes you think so? Don't you want the job?'

'Wantin' and gettin' are two different things,' Billy answered, slowly. 'Look, Mr Trumbull, you did me a favour. As big a favour as a man can do for another. I'm grateful. Too grateful to make trouble for you.'

'Trouble for me?' Trumbull drew on his pipe, and the reddish glow lighted his face. 'I don't understand.'

'I asked you for the job thinkin' maybe I'd get the chance to pay you back sometime for what you did for me. Maybe I was wantin' to show you that you didn't make no mistake savin' my neck from stretchin'. Either way, I didn't think it through. I've got a gun rep – that means I've killed men. The way it stands, I'll probably kill some more.'

Trumbull was silent for a moment, then the chair squeaked as he leaned forward and knocked out the dottle of his pipe against the porch rail. 'A year ago that would have horrified me, Billy,' he said, finally. 'Now I've learned to wait and see. A man learns to trust his own judgement out here – or nothing. Like I said, I've made mistakes before – and in men, too. I'll risk it this time.'

Billy's breath went out in an audible sigh. 'That's fair enough,' he said. 'If that was all there was to it. But it ain't. There's Ryan. You an' him are goin' to tangle. If you don't know that, you're a damn fool. An' hirin' me is like you slappin' Ryan in the face. I'll ask it plain, Mr Trumbull. Did you figger it out that way – an' hire me to ride for you thinkin' I'd take care of Ryan sooner or later?'

Again Trumbull didn't reply at once. The wicker chair protested as he crossed his legs. Then he said, 'The first time I ever saw Mr Ryan, he wanted to buy my interest in Horn for what I'd paid for it. He put it rudely, making it quite clear he didn't think I had the guts to run a working ranch. I refused. The second time I saw him, he informed me he would run my "ass" off Horn if I didn't change my tune. I'm a stubborn man, Billy. There is no man alive who can frighten me into doing what he wants me to do. The trouble I have with Ryan is of our own making; it has nothing to do with you. I expect nothing from you but an honest day's work.'

For a moment Billy remained silent, then he said, 'Thanks, Mr Trumbull.' He turned to go, but Trumbull's quiet voice stopped him.

'I'm curious, though, Billy. What if I told you I'd hired you only because I thought you would eventually shoot Ryan? What would you do?'

'I'd kill him tonight,' Billy said in his gentle, boy's voice. 'Goodnight, Mr Trumbull.'

Billy had reached the steps before Trumbull's odd-toned 'Goodnight,' reached him.

His soft footsteps faded into the night, and Harry Trumbull sucked on his cold pipe, thinking hard. Then a match exploded into brightness beyond the porch, and Pete Burnett's hawk-like face stood out. The Horn ramrod came up on the porch, sat on the low railing.

'Billy's real sudden-like,' he said, softly. 'And, unless he's funnin', he means exactly what he says. Just in case you're wonderin'.'

'I'm not,' Trumbull replied. He filled his pipe from an oilskin pouch, struck a match to light it. 'If it's a proper question, Pete, how long have you known the boy?'

'Most of his life,' Burnett answered. 'We grew up together in Santa Fe. His ma was a widow. Come from the East. I think I heard once Billy was born in New York. He was about five when I first seen him. Burned black as an Apache, his eyes lookin' like daylight through holes in a blanket. He was havin' a dust-up with a Mexican kid three-four years older than him. Billy was bein' licked bad. But he wouldn't holler "Uncle". Didn't even cry, an' his face was all bloody. I pulled the Mexican off'n him, an' Billy kept yellin' he'd kill him. That's all I got out of him. I carried him home to his ma. She took in washin' from Fort Sumner. When Billy was ten, he caught that Mexican kid an' like to beat him to death.'

Trumbull puffed on his pipe in silence. Burnett cleared his throat. 'When Billy was fourteen, he got into trouble. He always walked about two feet off the ground. He never saw what things were really like, always playin' make-believe. He still does. All kids play usin' sticks for guns, an' chasin' imaginary Indians. Most kids know deep down it's just pretend, but with Billy it was real. You could tell. Made it different. He was so busy livin' in his private places he didn't have time to see the real world. Mrs Bascom had it rough. The rest of us knew what she was doin', but Billy always played she was a lady an' never say anythin' else. One day Billy come home, an' a drunken soldier was just leavin' their shack. He patted Billy on the head an' told him his mother was the best whore in town.

'Billy kind of froze. All the brown seemed to run out of his face. He was shakin' all over. "Take that back!" he yelled, only it come out a kind of croakin' whisper. It made me sick to my stomach to hear it. It was the sound of all his dreams fallin' into pieces, just dirty mud after all. He kept yellin' it, over an' over, an' all that come out was this croakin' noise. The soldier laughed an' shoved Billy away from him. Billy tried to hit him, an' that soldier just plain beat the livin' hell out of him. I had to carry Billy into the shack where they lived. His mother had seen it, an' she tried to talk to him, but he turned his face to the wall an' laid on his bed, not movin' at all. I went home. We had a signal. Billy used to toss a rock against the wall of my room, an' we'd sneak out nights sometimes. I heard the rock that night an' come out, an' there was Billy. He was just fourteen, an' smaller than most kids his age. He said, real quiet-like, "I'm leavin', Pete, for good. But first I'm goin' to settle with that army bastard." I tried to talk to him, but it was no good. I followed him into town. He knew where he was goin'. There was a cantina where soldiers hung out, an' this same drunken cavalryman was there. I stayed outside the door, but I could see what went on. Billy walked into that saloon, an' called the soldier every dirty name in the book. The soldier took a swing at him, an' Billy dodged back an' pulled a knife. I'd seen him usin' it to whittle with before – reckon he stole it someplace. It had a good seven-inch blade, an' Billy had honed it to a razor edge, like a hog-sticker. "Now, you filthy bastard, tell the truth!" he whispered. "Tell me you lied about my mother. Go on, say it!" The soldier looked kind of taken back, then he laughed. "Your mother's a whore, you dirty little half-breed!" he yelled, an' the room was so quiet you could hear the wind touchin' the walls. Billy held there, lookin' sick, kind of swayin'. Then he moved like a strikin' rattler. His knife disappeared, ripped in an' up. The soldier let out a squawk an' grabbed at his belly an' Billy danced back. He wasn't scared now. He was livin' a different kind of dream, an' likin' it. I could hear him laughin'. "Burn in hell for a rotten liar!" he whispered, an' then before anybody in the saloon could get their wits together he backed out through the door. "Goodbye, Pete," he said to me, an' then run off.'

30

Burnett paused to flip his cigarette away. 'The kid was sixteen, an' growed up when I seen him again. It was in El Paso. He'd spent the two years in Mexico. How he lived an' what he done nobody knows, but there's been ugly talk. He come back a top hand with a horse, an' drivin' a string of cows ahead of him. He sold 'em for what he could get, an' tried his hand at livin' high for a week. That's how long his money lasted. He got in trouble with a gambler, shot him dead, an' rode out of town one jump ahead of the marshal. Since then he's kept on the move. I heard about him in Arizona, Texas, an' Mexico again – each time when he killed a man. Sometimes he works, an' sometimes he doesn't. When he doesn't, he ain't fussy about what brand a cow's wearin'. But then, who is? Old John Chisum made his start with borrowed cows. Ryan's not better. Forty years ago, after the Mexicans got run out of Texas, the rule was cows belonged to the first man that got to 'em. It ain't a hell of a lot different now.'

'I'm beginning to think so, myself,' Trumbull agreed, quietly. 'I've asked a lot of the wrong questions, Pete. I know that. Still, I've tried to understand, to avoid making a complete fool of myself. But the time has come when questions have piled high without answers. At risk of angering you, I've got to ask them.'

The Horn ramrod shifted position on the rail. 'Loose talk an' pointed questions are discouraged out here. With a friend you over-look the first and answer the second.'

'Thank you, Pete. That makes it easier for me. I understand a man like Ryan. There are men of his stripe in every country. Horn is a business proposition with me – I'm a boot-black cowman, as you call them out here. What may be more difficult for you to under-stand is the fact Horn has become more than dollars and cents to me. I consider it my home. I will spend the rest of my life here. But not at the cost of giving in to Ryan.'

'You wouldn't last long if you did,' came the laconic reply.

'Until today, I've discounted the bloody stories I've been told – not as untrue, but more as unreal. Those two hanged men were real, Pete.' Trumbull paused to relight his pipe. 'The first question is, would Ryan have hanged those men if he'd found them on

31

another property – say Howie Richards' Triple R?'

'Not without talkin' first to Richards.'

'That's about what I'd gathered.' Trumbull sighed heavily. 'It's plain enough that Ryan is contemptuous of me.'

'Not as much as he was this mornin',' Pete cut in, quietly. 'An' hirin' Billy will put another rock in his craw.'

'Billy. It's strange that one man – only a boy, really – should be so important to others.'

'Not important, just dangerous. Ryan wouldn't believe you hired the kid because you was thinkin' of Billy Bascom. That ain't the way Ryan reasons. He'll figger you butted in just to draw the line. Now he'll know you'll push back. If he's disappointed, he won't show it. To his way of lookin' at it, hirin' Billy is your way of sayin' if he wants trouble you're ready to dish it out.'

'You say that as if you were pleased,' Trumbull said, musingly. 'Perhaps you're right. The second question is more serious. How far will Ryan go? What trouble can I expect?'

'Maybe none.' Burnett paused. 'Maybe plenty. Range wars usually start slow an' are pure hell to stop. You got water an' land. Ryan wants them. But I got a funny feelin' it's more than just that with Jason Ryan. More than anything else, he wants to stay top man here in Lanyard County. He'll do one of two things: he'll walk soft an' wait it out, or he'll put the pressure on. Things like cuttin' fences, stampedin' gather herds. You take 'em without hittin' back, he'll go further, tryin' to make you pull in your horns. In the cow business, a man can go broke sudden-like. In your case, Ryan will try to hurry it up.'

'And if I push back, like for like?'

'Maybe Ryan will back down.' Burnett's voice was openly dubious.

'But if he doesn't?' Trumbull persisted.

Pete Burnett stood up, a tall, strong figure against the night sky. 'Then, Mr Trumbull, we got a war, a real war, on our hands.'

CHAPTER 3

Conchita Noriega awakened at the touch of the hot sun through the small, high window set in the eastern wall of the posada, and almost instantly felt the aliveness of the moment. At sixteen, Conchita was a full-grown woman by frontier standards; indeed, her mother had begun to remark about the fact that she had not as yet seriously considered any of the many men who found her to their liking. The principal problem lay in the fact that half-breed Mexican-Apache girls, while a cut above squaws, still had few claims to respect on the part of the young gringos of the town. Her mirror told her each day that the dark beauty lavished upon her as a gift of her Apache gods was her chief asset, and one that would not last forever. At twenty, most Indian and Mexican women had gone to fat. The thought brought a quick, anxious frown between her perfectly arched bows, and Conchita came out from under the light covers of the bed in a single bound.

On slender brown feet she danced across the room to the tarnished mirror over her battered dresser. She considered her reflection gravely, the high lift of her full, round breast, the flat perfection of her stomach, and the slender suppleness of her hips beneath the flimsy cambric gown she wore. For a moment she studied herself, then, with a slight frown, stepped out of the gown and pirouetted about in front of the mirror, her arms raised behind and above her in the classic stance of the Spanish dance.

Entranced with her own image and thoughts, Conchita did not hear the slight scuffling at the high window nor notice the shadow that darkened the narrow embrasure. A boy's soft laughter sounded, and, with a startled gasp, Conchita whirled, snatched up her gown and held it before her. A man's lean legs swung into the room, and he dropped lightly to the floor. Anger, not fright, stirred her dark features for a moment, then she gasped again.

'Billito!'

Billy Bascom grinned and made a mock bow. 'Me, *amada mia!*'

The girl came into his arms, and her kiss was warm and

passionate before she remembered her nakedness and drew back. 'Am I a *puta* of the town to be visited this way?' She backed away from him. 'Close your eyes. You've seen too much already.'

'Never mind, *amada*,' Billy replied, but obediently closed his eyes. His boyish face sobered. 'I'm sorry it's been so long. I came when I could.'

In one tigerish movement she donned the gown, drew a heavy silk mantilla about her shoulders, and sat on the edge of the bed. 'Is it so difficult to ride in to Lanyard to see me, then?'

'Not difficult, just dangerous,' Billy answered. He opened his eyes and came toward her. 'I've changed, Conchita, but it's harder being honest that I thought it would be.'

'A change?' Her eyebrows lifted in mockery. 'When the sun rises in the west, when the stars stop shining, then will you change! Does the wind change and become a cloud? Does the moon change and become the sun? Does ...'

He bent forward and kissed her, and her words trailed away. One brown arm encircled his neck, drew him down. For a moment their lips met and clung, and she surrendered utterly to him as his arms crushed her to him. Then with a laugh she pulled free, leaving the mantilla in his grasp.

'At least that does not change!' she whispered. He reached for her again, but she shook her head. 'No more. It is not the time. 'Rique will be coming to see why I'm late. Would you ruin my name?'

'I'd kill the man that tried to,' Billy answered softly. He leaned back across the bed, smiling. 'I had to make sure you had not forgotten me, *querida*.'

'Who forgets Billito?' Her black eyes considered him gravely. 'There has been wild talk: that you were almost hanged by Triangle; you had gone to work for the Englishman, Trumbull; you shot Bob Oringer. Always I listen, and wait for the time I will hear you are dead.'

He stood up. 'Not yet,' he said, softly. 'I didn't come here to talk.' He stepped closer to her, and she leaned against him. For a moment she pushed back from his embrace, studying his face.

34

Then her slim arms bent, went up and around his neck, drawing his face down to hers.

'I love you, Billy,' she whispered, her lips moving against his. 'You are not the first man I've known – probably not the last – but you are the one I will remember....'

A heavy step sounded in the hall, and there came a soft tap-tapping on her door. Conchita stiffened in his arms. One soft, brown hand came up and lay across his mouth.

A man's voice called, 'Conchita, it is I, Enrique. Let me come in, little one! I have news for you.'

'Go away, 'Rique,' she answered, impatiently. 'Leave me alone.'

'But, Conchita ...' the man's voice thinned to a pleading whine. 'It has been a long time since you have laughed with me, let me touch you....'

'Not half so long as the next time, *cabrón*!' she flashed. 'Now go away. I am not dressed yet. I will be out soon.'

'There is news,' Enrique insisted. 'News you will want to hear. It is about Billito. Señor Oringer just rode in, Triangle men with him. They are looking for Billito.'

Conchita felt Billy tense, but his smile did not change. 'I have not seen him in weeks,' the girl replied. 'I am not interested. He is nothing to me.'

'But they have found his horse, here in Lanyard. They are waiting for him....'

Conchita spun around. 'I said I am not interested in your old woman's tales!' she yelled fiercely. 'Leave me alone before I tell Maria you are after me again. You remember the last time...?'

There was silence on the other side of the door, then slow, heavy steps reluctantly withdrawing. She turned back to Billy. 'They've waited for you to ride into Lanyard. They knew you would come....'

Billy smiled and came toward her. 'Then let them wait a little longer,' he said, gently, and his arms drew her to him.

Billy awakened suddenly, stretched, smiled, then opened his eyes. The room was getting dark; the sun had set, and the evening breeze was beginning to cool the adobe walls. Billy scratched his sweaty chest, half-turned to put an arm across the other side of the bed, then drew it back, disappointed; Conchita was gone. He frowned and sat up, swinging his legs off the side of the bed. He found his shirt hanging from one brass newel, and pulled out his pack of tobacco. He made his cigarette, then a match flared in the growing darkness, and he sucked the acrid smoke deeply into his lungs.

He could hear music from the cantina at the front of the building, the murmur of men's voices broken now and then by shrill laughter and the clatter of pans in the kitchen. A girl's voice lifted above the other sounds in a song. He listened to the soft Spanish words, the humming twang of a guitar, and smiled in the darkness. Conchita – she sang as gracefully as she walked. The song ended, and men clapped loudly. The noise from the main room of the cantina grew louder as a door was opened, softened as it closed again. High heels clattered sharply against the tiled floor outside, then the door to the room opened, and he heard the rasp of a bolt being shut when it was closed again.

She came to him in the darkness of the room. She wore a heavy perfume, and her body was a warm, live pressure in his arms. Her seeking lips found his, and her hands rumpled his hair, dug sharply into his naked body, For a long moment they held there, bound by the strength of their passion, and then Conchita drew back, breathing hard through parted lips.

'*Bastante!*' she whispered. 'Enough! You've got to go, Billito, now! Bob Oringer is here in the cantina – half the Triangle crew is in town.'

Billy kissed her again, gently. 'Reckon you're right.' He turned back to the bed, found his shirt, pulled it on. The girl waited in silence, then she asked, 'Where is your gun, Billy?'

His soft laughter sounded. 'Forgot it.'

'As quickly as you'd forget your left arm,' she returned. 'Don't joke with me, Billy.'

'I told you I'd changed.' There was self-mockery in his voice. 'At least I'm makin' my try. Triangle ain't helpin' me much.'

'Why do you want to change?'

36

He was silent for an instant, then a match flared as he lit a new cigarette. He studied her face in the match light. 'Maybe I figger it's time I put down some roots.' The match went out, and darkness closed about them.

Her voice held an odd note he had never heard before. 'We cannot change what we are, Billy. Sometimes I, too, have wished … But it is foolish. I will grow old and fat and ugly like Maria, and you – there is only one end for you, Billy.'

'A gun or a rope,' he said, and laughed softly again. 'Odds are you're right, but it's fun to take a chance. What have I got to lose?'

Before she could reply, a door banged, and feet thudded down the corridor beyond the room. Spur rowels jingled, then a heavy hand pounded on the door.

'What's keepin' you, baby?' a man's gruff voice called.

Conchita felt Billy stiffen as he recognized Bob Oringer's voice. 'There are still times I wish I was packin' a gun,' he said. His lips brushed hers fiercely. 'I'll be back when I can, *amada*!' he promised, then raised his voice to shout, 'Give Ryan my love, Oringer!'

Even as Billy sprang toward the window, going up in one lithe bound, there sounded a hard curse, and a shoulder drove savagely against the door. Conchita drew back against the wall as a gun barked and lead smashed the bolt that held the door. It flew back with a crash, and the heavy-shouldered figure of Bob Oringer hurtled into the room. His revolver lanced red flame, and the stink of black powder filled the room. Bullets shattered the high window, but Billy Bascom's laughter rang out from beyond it.

Oringer balanced awkwardly, his right leg stiff, then came toward the girl, his face twisted with rage 'You dirty little bitch, hidin' him in your room.' He raised his right arm to strike her, and Conchita swayed forward toward him, her right hand extended. Oringer caught the deadly gleam of steel, and jumped crazily back before the knife in her hand could rip into him.

'Damn you!' he gasped.

'You're too late, Señor – I was damned the moment I was born!'

Oringer held very still, staring at her, and slowly his anger faded, replaced by his slow, twisted grin. 'Never saw the wildcat that wasn't worth tamin'. I'll enjoy the job.'

'A cat has only one master,' she answered, tauntingly.

'At a time, you mean.' Oringer kept grinning. 'We'll see.' He swung around, limping as he moved. At the door he paused. 'You'll cry when Billy's laid in the ground – but you can't cry forever.'

He went out, and Conchita drew back against the wall, breathing hard. Then Enrique's thick-middled figure came through the doorway. He was sweating, and for once too agitated to take advantage of finding her alone.

'*¡Madre de Dios!*' he wheezed. 'Must you take for your lover the wildest one of all? Is it not enough these gringo dogs fight and raise hell every night, but you must set them to shooting each other over you?'

'Do not worry, *gordo*!' she returned angrily. 'Worry when these gringo dogs do not come, and the silver stops jingling in your pocket!' She spun about, her full skirt whirling about her slender brown legs. Her high, red heels clicked sharply as she went past him toward the cantina.

Pete Burnett came off the ridge, circled the far end of a deep coulee, and put his mount to the steep upward slope beyond. South of the brakes, where the jumbled, broken land ran across the base of the Halos, the Horn drift fence was a strangely green stripe across the brown hide of the earth, where matted grass clustered to the meagre moisture stored by the dried posts. Burnett rode around the far end of the fence, then followed the line of it across the face of the brakes. It ended where a shale ledge formed a natural wall, began again beyond.

He looked older and harder than his twenty-four years. He was a tall, angular man with a firm set to his jaw and grim lines about his mouth, which fought an endless battle with the soft humour of his blue eyes. A product of the same environment that had produced Billy Bascom and a thousand others of his stripe, Pete Burnett differed from all of them in one essential way. He had never found a reason strong enough to make him kill another man.

Just the same, he was too intelligent not to know the time would

most likely come, and he had approached the problem of mas-
tering his revolver in the same methodical way he did most other
things. He had known the advantages of a fast draw before he was
ten years old – and had recognized the inherent weakness of it.
A too-hasty shot usually missed. So he had set himself the task of
learning to be accurate first. The fast draw could wait. The end
result satisfied him; he couldn't match the blinding speed of men
like Billy Bascom, but the man didn't live who could place five shots
more accurately than Pete Burnett. And his incredible accuracy
served a double purpose; it was tangible evidence that the first man
he fired at was certain to die, and this, in turn, gave pause to those
inclined to settle arguments with lead. At least, he thought darkly,
until now....

Topping a final rise, the brakes behind him, Burnett reined
in. His eyes narrowed as they followed the line of the drift fence
across the open range. Designed to turn back Horn cattle from the
canyons and arroyos of the Halos, it was one more innovation that
Trumbull had introduced on the sprawling ranch. He noted the
smudge of smoke against the flat horizon where the work wagon
had paused for the noonday meal. His blunt thumb scraped the
angle of his jaw. It was Trumbull's intent to run the fence to Three
Waters, some ten miles east, and for half that distance it would
parallel Ryan's Triangle land. A man with good sense would see
that the drift fence would work both ways, to keep the cows out
of the coulees and brakes at the same time holding both spreads
apart; but since when had Ryan been such a man? The line between
Burnett's blue eyes deepened.

The shimmering heat devils danced in front and to both sides
as he rode on. At least, he reflected grimly, the damn wind wasn't
making a man eat dust twenty hours a day. That would come later,
just before the brief, hard winter rains. The heat would ease when
they came, but a man afoot would walk in gumbo mud to his butt.
For the ten-thousandth time in his life, Burnett cursed the land,
and yet knew inside he would not leave if he could. A man needed
something to take his measure, to make him come fully alive; for
some, like the kid, a gun and another man to face was enough. For

Pete Burnett, it took more. The hell of it was, the time would come when he would have to choose once and for all between his own hard way and the more violent path of the kid – and that time was coming soon, too damn soon.

The men were squatted about the chuck wagon eating their meal when Burnett rode up. The cook, a grizzly-whiskered man, was bent over the open fire, stirring the big iron kettle suspended there. He straightened and parted his thick moustache to spit to one side.

'Howdy, Pete,' he hailed Burnett and dished slumgullion into a plate, held it out. Burnett eyed the string of horses to one side as he rode in, and the frown was between his eyes as he dismounted. He came up to the fire, accepted the tin plate of food, and stirred sugar into a crockery mug of black coffee. He carried the plate and cup into the shade of the wagon, nodding to the four men hunkered down there.

Vaughn Morgan sat half under the wagon bed, his bony knees drawn up before him, the plate resting across them. 'Come to change the kid's diapers, Pete?' he asked.

Burnett didn't smile. None of the others laughed at the hard joke. Billy Bascom was seated on the wagon tongue, his plate in his lap. His colourless eyes went to Morgan almost lazily, and his half-smile went into place.

'You keep asking for trouble, Morgan,' Burnett said, quickly, 'you're goin' to find it.'

'I thought it was funny,' the tall man said.

Oscar Wiggin was leaning against one wheel. He laughed scornfully. 'Like hell,' he cut in. 'If'n I was the kid, I'd skin you an' hang your hide on my wall.'

Vaughn Morgan glared at the fat-faced rider. He wiped his mouth with the back of his hand. 'Maybe you'd like the job?' he demanded, truculently.

'Try ridin' me, you skinny bastard, an' you'll find out!' Wiggin flared. 'Why don't you lay off, Morgan? Ryan payin' you to make trouble on Horn?'

Morgan's plate went into the dirt, and he came up like a

diamondback uncoiling. Burnett stepped quickly in front of him. 'Drop it,' he ordered, flatly. He watched Morgan's eyes. The man was thinking fast, balancing things only he knew in his mind. Then he grinned. The expression was as false as his too-quick anger, Burnett thought.

'All right, so I'm a grouchy son of a bitch,' Morgan said. 'Runnin' this crazy fence across the ass-end of nowhere is enough to drive a man loco.'

'It's still a free country,' Burnett said shortly. 'You can get your time just by askin' for it.'

Morgan's smile remained fixed. 'I said I was just grouchin'. Forget it.' He walked away with his loose-limbed stride.

Wiggin watched him go, and spat contemptuously, then lifted his cup. He drained it, then groaned. 'When you figger we're runnin' this damn fence into Chicago? I feel like I been stretchin' wire most of my growed-up life.'

Burnett walked over to the kid. 'Hear you had a ruckus in town last night.'

'Nothin' to it, Pete. I ain't killed nobody.'

'Yet,' Burnett amended soberly. 'Where's your horse, Billy?'

Billy Bascom wiped the bottom of his plate with the last of his bread, chewed carefully and swallowed before replying. 'Did a little horse-swappin',' he said. 'Even up. No boot.'

'There's a Triangle horse on the string. You ride it out from town?'

Billy sighed resignedly. 'Yep. It's Bob Oringer's. Go ahead, Pete, give me hell for it.'

Burnett sat on the wagon tongue and began to eat. He paused between bites to study the other's youthful face. 'You're a hard man to figger, Billy.'

'I avoided trouble, Pete. I walked soft an' the long way around. I'll keep doin' it. Oringer rode into town. He was primed for it, but I wanted no part. He took my mare, an' I returned the favour. That's it. I wasn't even wearin' hardware.' Billy frowned. 'I'll take his horse back, but you'll have your trouble dumped in your lap, because it's a cinch bet I'd never ride out of Triangle alive.'

'I know that, too,' Burnett answered. 'But if you don't take the horse back, Oringer will come after it – and there's the trouble again. Doesn't matter much who started it, once it's rollin'.'

'You can't keep headin' it off, Pete,' Billy declared, then straightened as he caught the hard drum of running hoofs and heard Oscar Wiggin's sharp warning.

'Company comin'! It's Triangle, an' they're loaded for bear!'

CHAPTER 4

Billy stood up slowly, watching Pete Burnett's face. Burnett's eyes darkened and narrowed; otherwise no expression showed.

'I want no trouble,' he warned. 'I'll do the talking.'

Burnett spoke to all of them, but Billy was aware that the words were primarily directed at himself, and his smile changed to a grin. He slumped back against the wagon bed and began to build a cigarette between his nimble fingers. He struck a match against the iron tyre of the wheel and lit the smoke.

Dust stood up in a column against the flat horizon, slowly bending under the pressure of a vagrant breeze. Seven riders came ahead of it, the pride of being Triangle men stiffening their backs and lending them an arrogant air. It was most evident in the manner of the man who led them, and his followers rode carefully a stride behind him.

'King Ryan the First,' Billy murmured, then fell silent as Burnett's swift, hard glance shot to him.

The Triangle riders pulled up, the dust of their passage raining over the still figures of the men of Horn. Ryan rose in his stirrups to stare back along the line of fence, and then walked his horse around the end post toward the chuck wagon. His lean, dark face betrayed no emotion. Bob Oringer rode close behind Ryan, his expression wary.

Ryan stopped his horse and singled out Burnett with his eyes.

'This has been open range for more than twenty years,' he said, slowly. 'When that is changed, I want to be told about it.'

'You knew about it five minutes after the first posthole was dug,' Burnett answered. 'Look, Jason, we're grown-up men.'

'A man can try to grow too big,' Ryan returned, flatly. 'I've gone along with Trumbull's outsider's ways. I've taken things from him I wouldn't from a Westerner. I'll take no more.'

Burnett waited patiently and then decided he'd had enough. 'Every foot of this fence is on Horn land. You ran a drift fence across the north end of the brakes ten years ago. You were damned for it, but you ran it just the same. Within a year, half the range in the county had the rough places fenced off.'

Ryan listened without a change of expression. 'I'm not talking about what I did ten years ago, I'm talking about what you're doing now. Trumbull is a stranger with strange ways, but you know better, Burnett. This is the second time you've meddled in Triangle business. There won't be a third time. I'm tired of your hiding behind the Englishman's dud front.'

Billy felt a singing tension building inside himself. The Triangle owner was trouble-hunting, and it would have been Billy's way to see he found it sudden-like. But Burnett held rock still.

'Triangle cows have drifted through here into the brakes for years,' he said, slowly. 'You've lost cattle and money; this fence will stop it. But it isn't the fence that's eatin' on you, Jason. You want every man you meet to knuckle under to you. Now it's my turn. All right, I'll do it just once.' His face remained set and hard. 'This drift fence will work to the advantage of both Triangle and Horn. Mr Trumbull would like to run it to Three Waters. Since it edges both ranches, Mr Trumbull would like your help maintaining it.'

Ryan listened, his eyes narrowing with anger. 'You're talking like a fool. How long do you think Trumbull's fence will stand?'

Pete Burnett's manner changed, subtly. His tall, angular frame seemed to slacken as if tension had withdrawn from him. He turned to look at the Triangle riders, studied the faces one by one, then looked down the length of fence. He squinted up at the sky. 'This is a dry land,' he said, quietly. 'At a rough guess, I'd say that fence was good for a hundred years.'

Anger ran harsh lines down either side of Ryan's face. For an instant he sat there, then wheeled his horse. 'Tear it down, Bob!' he ordered.

Billy saw Oringer's broad grin, then Burnett's voice, suddenly as brittle as the crash of glass, cut in, 'I told you I'd knuckle down just once, Ryan.' His right arm crooked, and his hand rested on his holstered revolver. 'You're on Horn land. Get off.'

Bob Oringer froze. He darted a swift look at Ryan. The Triangle owner was facing away from Burnett, and his back stiffened. He had made a mistake and pushed this man too far.

Burnett said, 'Turn your horse around, Jason, slow.'

Ryan obeyed. Burnett hadn't moved. 'There is no reason for trouble,' he said. 'Trumbull doesn't want it, and I don't want it.' Without warning, Burnett's right hand blurred, and his revolver came out and cracked. A chunk of wood flew from the nearest fence post. 'The next one's yours, Jason, if you want it.'

Pete Burnett still stood indolently at ease, his revolver loosely in his hand. Billy thought, my God, he's fast! And knew the same thought had slammed home to Ryan and his men.

The anger lines on Ryan's face faded, and his features became stone-like. 'There will be other times,' he said, slowly.

'None better than now,' Burnett replied harshly.

Ryan sat very still, working hard on his thoughts behind the mask of his face. His eyes remained on Burnett's, trying to read any softness, or weakness, there. He found none and raised his head to look pointedly away. Without speaking, he shook his head in a strangely final way, lifted his hands slowly and turned his horse.

'Just a minute.' Burnett's voice remained flat of tone. Ryan halted his horse. 'Tell Oringer to get off the kid's mare. His own horse is on the string.'

Ryan didn't turn. 'Do as he says,' he ordered.

Billy saw the frown on Bob Oringer's face, caught the dark look he threw in his direction and grinned back. In silence the Triangle ramrod dismounted, unsaddled the mare. He walked to the string of Horn horses, found his own and led him out. He saddled with angry speed, and even as he finished, Jason Ryan walked his horse out of camp, past the end of the fence. The other Triangle riders wheeled their horses to follow. They had lost face by Ryan's refusal to fight, and their angry resentment shone in their eyes. Oringer stared fixedly at Billy Bascom for an instant, then swung into the saddle and spurred his horse. Dust fell in his wake in thick, blinding curtains.

Somewhere in the murk a shouted curse carried back to them then the drum of hoofs faded away. Billy, watching Burnett, saw the easy indolence drain away, replaced by a strange air of disappointment. There were harsh lines in Burnett's face, and his eyes were bitter.

Oscar Wiggin came up, his fat face grinning. 'That's tellin' the old bastard!' he yelled. 'That's the end of that.'

Billy followed the receding cloud of dust with narrowed eyes. Like hell! he thought. Now it begins.

Jason Ryan's inclination, facing Pete Burnett, had been to ride the man down, to smash anything that stood in his way, but he had curbed it ruthlessly, and apart from a slight irritation, felt no regret. Twenty years ago, Pete Burnett would be dead now, his camp burned, his fence destroyed. But times change, and only fools didn't change with them.

Bob Oringer spurred his mount abreast that of the rancher. His half-moon face was sullen, the insolence he usually kept hidden from Ryan showing through. 'That was a hell of a play,' he said flatly.

Ryan didn't turn his head. He was aware of the rage that filled the other man. There was a raw viciousness in Oringer that sometimes disturbed Ryan, and to curb it, force it back, was a kind of game of which he never tired. He was aware, too, of Oringer's insane hatred of Billy Bascom and had placed it into his plans. With that blind, unreasoning anger filling him, Oringer could be turned to Ryan's own uses. He didn't reply now, but rode in silence, letting Oringer's sullenness grow.

Like many big men, Jason Ryan rode, not as a part of his horse, but dominating it, subjecting it to his will. He preferred vicious horses and broke them in his own way; and no mount lasted him long, for when their spirit died he took another. So when his horse shied and began to pitch, Ryan tightened his grip on the reins, and rode out the spell expressionlessly. When the horse tired, he raked his rowels across its withers and forced it to a killing run in the pressuring heat.

It was a violent release from the tensions that had built inside him, and when, at last, the horse stumbled and fell into a shambling walk and would not respond to the bite of his spurs, Ryan eased back in the saddle, his face reddened from the effort expended in the heat of the day. A strange feeling of satisfaction filled him. He relaxed his grip on the reins and allowed the animal to pick its own pace. He looked back; his men were strung out behind him, not pushing their horses hard, but following.

Oringer rode up first, round face red and sweating. Jason Ryan had lit a cigar and was looking off into the red-yellow distance. 'Get me another horse,' Ryan ordered. 'Then tell the others to ride in. I want to talk to you.'

Ryan dismounted, letting the reins trail in the dirt. He walked a few paces away, a sombre giant of a man, dominating even the harsh land about him. Grama grass and soapweed lay in scattered clumps to the far horizon where the brown smudge of hills lifted against the colourless sky. He heard Oringer giving orders, then the muted thud of hoofs. Dust rose slowly.

'Here's Martin's horse,' Oringer said and, when the bigger man turned, he made an attempt to mask the sullenness in his face and eyes.

'You hate my guts, don't you, Bob?' Ryan asked. 'Don't bother lying – I don't give a damn what you think.'

Oringer scowled, then spat to one side. 'I don't pretend to understand you, Jason,' he said, slowly. 'But seein' you back down to Pete Burnett is hard to swallow.'

'You can't see beyond the end of your nose,' Ryan cut in, sharply. 'Your gun rep is all that matters to you. Never back down, never give in – blind, stupid pride that shoves you straight into an early grave.' He frowned and looked away. 'Without it, you'd be worth nothing to me. I have to depend upon men like you. For that reason it has become important that you understand what you see, that you think before you let your damn pride take you to hell.'

Ryan's blue eyes stared into the brown immensity about them, tracing the movement of a distant dust whorl, the scattered grey, thin clouds over the dark line of mountains to the west. 'This is a big land,' he said, slowly. 'And I own or control most of it. But no land is big enough for a truly ambitious man, because his ambition grows faster than any possible realization of it. It is this way with me. And it is growing harder to keep what you have. But the man who keeps it these next ten years will own it forever. Right now Trumbull is in my way, and I'm going to knock him out of it. Trumbull and Swenson and anyone else who stands with them. But I'm going to do it my own way, in my own time, and I'm taking no chances. Law is coming to Lanyard County. It is going to be *my* law – bought and paid for.'

'With Trumbull hirin' guns like Billy Bascom, maybe it'll get here in time to see you get a good funeral,' Oringer returned, grimly. 'Hell, ten years ago I could figger you, Jason. Now I can't. You look like the same man, but sure as hell don't act like the same one.'

That hardness of Ryan's face didn't change. 'I came into this country with a hundred head of cows and one thin dime in my pocket. I've still got the dime. Over the years a lot of men have stood in my way, and most of them are buried on Triangle land. But what I did without thinking about twice twenty years ago would bring the whole country down on my back today. The way it used to be, a man with twenty riders in his hire could buck against anything he met. Now I've got a hundred men, and have to walk soft.' His big hands clenched into knotted fists. 'But not for long.'

He stood very still, his body expressing the rocklike strength that was his. The harsh land lay about him, sullen and brooding, but dominated by him. For an instant he remained silent, sensing this, letting the satisfaction of it fill him, then he turned away. 'Two men are waiting for me at the house. One of them is the governor of the territory by presidential appointment. The other is Jem Mace who will be named sheriff tomorrow. I own them both, Oringer. They're going to see just one side of what happens here in Lanyard County – my side. I'm going to smash anyone who gets in my way – smash him to a bloody pulp. And those two men will make it legal. There are a lot of bigwigs in this country, from the president on down – and every one of them has his own row to hoe. New Mexico is a big land – and there'll be one big man out here they'll all suck up to for support. That man's going to be me.' He broke off to stare into Oringer's eyes. 'Maybe you've got ambitions, Bob. Maybe you'd like to throw a longer shadow. Like being made Jem Mace's deputy for instance – and still draw down your Triangle pay.'

Oringer blinked, then slowly he grinned.

For a moment Ryan watched him, then he nodded. He turned to the horse that Oringer had brought and stepped up to the saddle. 'All right, now you know. I'm riding in. You're not. I don't want an open fight with Trumbull or his men – not yet. But if that fence is standing tomorrow morning you're through!'

Ryan held there for an instant, then wheeled his horse and sent it off at a run. Oringer remained still. He frowned after the Triangle owner for moment, squinting his eyes, then spat again on the ground.

Bob Oringer was not a man to plan ahead, but direct action he understood, even when its appearance must be masked. He considered the problem for a full minute, then slowly began to grin. Deputy sheriff, he thought; not bad for a saddle bum who liked to look upon the better things. Conchita, for instance.... He licked his lips. Ryan would climb high and he'd need help. Oringer knew the kind he would need. His right hand touched his holstered Colt.

Billy Bascom had been a high rider too long to ever lose the habit of sleeping like a cat. Just as his unconscious gesture of hitching his gun belt over his hip persisted even after weeks of not wearing his weapon, it marked the difference between him and normal men. He fell into a soft doze a dozen times that night, only to start awake for no reason he could name. He leaned up on one elbow and listened to the night sounds: the soft snoring of Wiggin and the cook, the distant yapping of a coyote in the hills and an answer from the opposite direction. The horses of the remuda stirred restlessly. The wind made a soft, soughing sound through the canvas-covered bows of the chuck wagon. He was lying in his bedroll beneath it and he sat up, cross-legged, his head just touching the wagon bed, to roll a cigarette.

A sound reached him and died away before he could be sure it was the distant drumming of hoofs. He tensed as he heard the sand-muffled tread of a man's booted feet. Bright moonlight flooded the camp, and he saw the twin shadows of a man's legs walking close beside the wagon. He recognized Vaughn Morgan's tall, thin figure, started to speak, then remained still. Morgan was walking carefully, making almost no sound, and there was a wary tautness about him that he could feel. He heard Morgan reach his bedroll some distance away; there were muffled sounds. Puzzled, Billy rolled over to the edge of the moonlight. Morgan was kneeling, making up his bedroll. He straightened, lifted it, and walked past the wagon toward the string of horses.

Billy came lightly to his feet. 'Goin' some place?' he called out.

The other man halted, twisted about. He seemed almost frightened, but his voice sounded normally gruff. 'I'm quittin' this two-bit outfit,' he answered. 'I've had a bellyful of Pete Burnett – and you, too.'

'You always ride out in the middle of the night?' Billy asked, sharply.

Morgan seemed to hesitate for a fraction of an instant. 'I don't want no trouble. I figgered on bein' back at Horn come sun-up to draw my pay.'

Billy frowned. His sharp eyes moved around the camp; everything was as usual. Despite the feeling of alarm that ran through him, he could think of no reason to force Morgan to stay. 'Go ahead, ride out,' he said reluctantly.

Morgan spun around and resumed his way toward the remuda. He singled out his own horse, saddled it, lashed his bedroll behind the saddle, then stepped up. Abruptly his manner changed. He shook his fist toward Billy and yelled, 'I'll see you in hell, you mangy bastard!' He wheeled the horse and set it away at a run.

Until the hoofbeats died out, Billy stood still, and then he circled the camp twice, even past the end of the fence line. He stopped to listen for long minutes, but heard nothing. When he returned to his blankets under the wagon he remained awake for an hour, a nagging worry in the back of his mind evading his efforts to analyze it. At length he forced himself to lie back and relax, and sleep came with unexpected suddenness.

He dreamed of the rolling noise of thunder over the hills and awakened to the reality of the terrifying sound of a stampeding herd. Cold fear shot through him, and he half-arose, then fell back as the bawling cries of a running herd sounded almost upon him. It was black night, the moon having set, and the false dawn not yet lighting the eastern horizon. The paralyzing din of stampeding cattle is the most frightening of all sounds to a cattleman; the insane stupidity of the animals carrying them in a flesh-and-bone tide of destruction that only halts when turned in upon itself or run out.

Thick, roiling dust clogged the air. The bawling cries of cattle suddenly changed to pain-filled bellows, and the thrum of hoofs slowed, milled. The herd had struck the fence. Billy could imagine the mad scene taking place there in the blackness: the rolling eyes, tossing horns, the intolerable pressure of those behind forcing the leaders into the ripping, tearing barbed wire. He heard the high-pitched twang as the wires broke. He was moving, trying to get to his feet. He heard a man yell something from the darkness and then a sudden, shrill scream that was abruptly cut off, and the wagon rocked under the impact of tons of living flesh. The high, frightened shrilling of horses cut through the sonorous bellowing of cattle. The horses of the remuda would be fighting to get free, to run before the menacing advance of the stampede. The wagon shifted sickeningly, started to tip, and Billy threw himself from under it as it went over with an earth-jarring crash. He fought the canvas tarp that fell about him, climbed into the bed of the wagon and braced his back and legs to stay there while the chuck wagon

50

pitched and tossed to the surging of maddened cows like a small boat in a wind-lashed sea.

For what seemed an eternity he held there, bruised and dazed, still unable to comprehend the nightmare that had struck without warning. The main body of the herd was past. Billy fell to the bottom of the up-ended wagon, amid a litter of broken crockery and metal pans. He heard the firmer sound of horses' hoofs, then the bitter, staccato barking of a revolver and a man's high-pitched, crazy laughter. The pounding hoofs surged past the camp and were gone.

Billy clambered slowly to his feet. Somehow he had received a cut across his forehead, and blood stung his eyes. He mopped at his head with a dust-grimed handkerchief. A few cows still milled about the wreckage of the camp, and the clogging dust was slowly settling.

'Oscar!' Billy called. 'Hey! Any of you guys make it?'

His voice sounded harsh and cracked. The distant bellowing of the still-running herd was his only answer. Billy cursed under his breath and stumbled forward. His feet struck something soft and giving, and he knelt, reached down. His hands touched something warm and wet, and jerked back. The dead man's body had been stomped into a jelly-like mass beneath the hoofs of the cattle. Billy turned away and was violently sick.

When the first, fierce red slice of the sun topped the hills to the east, Billy was patting dirt atop the last of three shallow graves. His face was streaked with sweat and dirt. Finished with the graves, he looked at the battered, overturned wagon, the trampled debris that was all that was left of the line camp. The last quarter-mile section of fence was gone, only one of the posts still upright. The gaunt, bleak land lay about him, oblivious to the tragedy that had been played out here. The affairs of men were too small, too transitory, for the bitter land to note their small affrays.

Billy stood still for a moment, bareheaded, facing the sun, his curly mop of hair grayed by dust. He raised his head and wished he knew a prayer, or even words to suit this moment of farewell. He hadn't known these men well; Oscar Wiggin had attracted him, and they might have become friends. The other men he had known hardly at all. He should have felt a sadness at their going, but all he had inside was a dull, burning rage. He had felt like this before, and each time he had killed a man. If he had known where to find Vaughn Morgan, he would have killed another.

Movement out on the prairie caught his attention, and he shaded his eyes. It was a horse, moving in closer, hesitantly. Despite the dust that covered it, he recognized his mare's red coat. The animal had come back, trying to find him. Some of the bitter anger faded, and Billy smiled his lopsided smile. His piercing whistle cut the silence, and he saw the horse veer toward the sound, whinnying an eager reply.

Billy dropped the shovel. He looked once more at the destroyed camp, at the low mounds of the graves, then pulled on his hat and walked to meet his horse.

CHAPTER 5

It took Jason Ryan less than five minutes to judge Winston Carlisle's character and reach a conclusion to his own satisfaction. Carlisle was a portly, big-bellied man who fared well and showed it. Despite rumours that President Hayes had appointed him governor of the Territory because of a lost bet, Carlisle had shown a surprising ability to make the office a profitable one for himself. While his favours did not come high, he granted them liberally and it was Ryan's private thought he would not last long. Still, Carlisle was in the saddle at the moment, and that was what was important.

A log-burning fireplace filled one side of the huge, adobe-walled living room of the Triangle ranch house, and a fire crackled there now. Each of the three men present in the room held a brandy glass and a fine cigar. The governor sat in a big wingback chair, legs extended toward the fire, his pot-belly thrusting out.

'... And the General laughed!' he finished the last of a long series of anecdotes about his Washington conquests in which his domination of President Hayes played a prominent part.

The third man was tall and lean, with a hatchet-sharp face divided into quarters by a beak-like nose and drooping yellow moustache. His face and hands betrayed his open-range origin, and his booted feet were proof he was still an active rider. He frowned into the fire, paying scant attention to the speaker. His name was Jem Mace, and he had been hand-picked by Ryan to be sheriff of Lanyard County.

'I can't see why Hayes has much to laugh about, considering his hard-money policy,' Ryan said, shortly. 'I've heard the Yankee greenback lovers took it hard – coming as it did on top of his kid-glove Southern policy.'

Carlisle coughed, his round face flushed. 'Just the same, Mr Ryan, let me assure you few men in this country exert the influence of Rutherford B. Hayes. True, he has his problems ...'

'The more, the better, as far as I'm concerned,' Ryan cut in. 'The harder they pull his nose in Washington, the less he'll be inclined to push it into affairs out here.'

Carlisle coughed again, and drained his brandy glass. He sighed heavily, like a cow blowing after water, to Ryan's mind, and stirred uneasily in the chair.

'That's blunt talk, Mr Ryan.'

'I'm a blunt man, Carlisle,' the rancher returned. He noticed that Jem Mace had straightened and was listening intently. 'I can be a hell of a lot blunter. You're an opportunist, and so am I. All right, there's a big pie to be cut up out here. But it's going to be messy. You're not going to like what happens. It's a cinch your Mr Hayes won't like it. Maybe he'll get upset – so upset he'll fire you right out of office. There's been talk he favours General Walton, anyhow.'

'Idle talk,' Carlisle blustered. 'Lew Walton is a story-book writer, a man who spends his time in dreaming up tales for the idle to read.'

'Lew Walton is the best shot in this country,' Ryan contradicted, flatly. 'He's rugged and he's smart. He's knocked around over the world. Don't let his fancy manner fool you. Underneath he's a curly-haired wolf with six-inch fangs. If he takes over the territory, he'll damned well ruin any chance of things being the way we want them.'

Carlisle mopped at his sweating face with trembling hands. 'I believe in being outspoken, Mr Ryan, but this ...'

'Scares you,' Ryan finished for him. 'I expected it to. That's why I'm laying it out for you. I'm going to take this territory. I'm going to ruin or kill every man who stands in my way. There'll be a stink that will reach Washington, but I intend it to reach it too late to stop me. To do this, I need your help. Badly enough to pay you more hard money than you ever saw before. No matter what I do, I'll be legally in the right. You'll see to that, as long as you last. And after I'm done you won't give a damn for Rutherford B. Hayes and his two-bit appointments. You'll need the rest of your life just to spend the interest on your money.'

Winston Carlisle was staring open-mouthed, but his jaws clamped abruptly upon his cigar, and the soft roundness of his face gave way to hard lines. 'All right, Ryan, you like it blunt. Have it that way. How much?'

Ryan blinked, then nodded. 'You've just erased my last doubts, Governor. You're the territorial government, and Jem Mace is the law in this county. I'm going to need you both. Mr Carlisle, there is one hundred thousand dollars on deposit in Santa Fe that will be transferred to your personal account tomorrow. With that as a start, how far can I go to get what I want?'

Carlisle stared at the ash-tipped end of his cigar, his face retaining the hard look. 'Five minutes after you effect that transfer, Mr Ryan, you can kill every other man in New Mexico, and I'll swear it was self-defence.'

Ryan picked up the brandy flask, poured liquor into each of the three glasses. He set the decanter down, raised his own glass. 'Gentlemen, I give you the Territory of New Mexico. One year from today it will be the largest single holding of any man on earth.'

Ryan drained his glass, then threw it to smash against the fireplace. A strange exultation seemed to light his carved rock features. 'May God have mercy on those in my way – for I'll have none.' His eyes moved to Carlisle's face. 'Tonight a beginning was made. A Triangle herd was stampeded through Trumbull's drift fence. Three Horn riders died under their hoofs. You break eggs to make an omelette, and you spill blood to win an empire. For thirty years I've heard talk about what a real range war would be like. Now we'll find out. When men like Lew Walton get around to writing the history of the West, they'll begin with the Lanyard County War.'

The afternoon sun glinted across the dust-filmed window of the room Harry Trumbull used for his office, and Trumbull turned away from it slowly to face the other two men present.

'I'm glad you're here, Nils,' he said, slowly. 'This will be your fight as much as mine.'

Nils Swenson nodded shortly. He was a sandy-browed man with a perpetually sunburned face that betrayed the fiery temper that so often plagued him. Only Jason Ryan had been in Lanyard County before him, and his Lazy S brand was carried by 10,000 head of cattle. His general store in Lanyard gave the Ryan-Dolan store it's only competition, and his hatred for Jason Ryan was the result of twenty years of accumulated incidents in which Ryan had always held the best of it. Although it set hard with him, the fact remained that his back had been against the wall until Trumbull's money had given him a new chance.

The grim-visaged Pete Burnett was the third man in the room, and Trumbull half-turned to face him. 'You say Billy buried them?'

'What was left of them.'

Trumbull frowned. 'It could not have been an accident?'

Burnett's bleak face broke into angry lines. 'It took three or four men half the night to round up the cattle and drive them in close. They knew what they were doing, and didn't give a goddamn – the number of cattle that barbed wire tore to pieces proves that. Only Billy's alley cat ways saved his life. He always keeps to himself.'

Trumbull nodded, reluctantly. 'You say Morgan cleared out before the stampede?'

Burnett's hard-lined mouth twisted. 'An hour or two before, according to Billy – which makes it pretty plain. Ryan kept Morgan on Horn to keep tabs on what you're doing. They figgered the cattle would finish off the whole crew, and Morgan could ride in today and explain what happened, and stick around to see what we did about it. Billy coming out of that hell alive must have been a shock to whoever was watching – and I figger it was Morgan. He'll have high-tailed it back to Triangle to let Ryan know what went wrong.'

Trumbull moved one hand over his face. 'Three men,' he said, slowly. 'My God, how can it be worth it to anyone?'

'It is to Ryan,' Burnett cut in, coldly. 'And a hundred more buried with them if it suits his purpose.'

With tired resignation, Trumbull slumped down into his swivel chair. 'I suppose you're right. But knowing it and proving it are two different things. With his record, Billy's testimony would be worthless.'

'That's just what I told Billy,' Burnett answered. 'Swenson will back up what I say. Ryan has waited a long time – now he's hit hard. There's a reason, and it's a simple one. He's got backing. If you had a thousand Holy Joes to testify, it wouldn't do one damn little bit of good.'

Swenson's angry face jerked in a nod. 'That's the hell of it. I've seen this coming. I tried to get to see Winston Carlisle, the new governor. I went clear to Santa Fe twice and got nothing but a run-around. Carlisle came into Lanyard yesterday afternoon. Nobody got a chance to talk with him because Triangle men surrounded him and hauled him off in Ryan's fancy rig. Jem Mace was with him – and it's two to one that Carlisle's naming Mace sheriff. The law is Ryan's law from here on in.'

'But there must be …' Trumbull stopped. Lines of strain made his face seem old.

'Most Westerners learn early in life that the only thing that will buck a cold deck is a fast gun,' Burnett said, grimly.

Trumbull's expressive face grew grave. 'It's incredible that in this day and age men must fight each other like animals – kill or be killed for domination of an area. How can it mean that much to any man?'

'Ryan isn't a man – he's a lobo wolf, slashing at anything that gets in his way. There is only one way to handle a lobo king – kill him before he ruins you.' Pete Burnett spoke slowly, heavily.

Swenson moved forward, his sharp jaw outthrust. 'Ryan will have his war, whether we want it or not. It's been coming to this for a long time. That's why I rode out here today. For months now, strange riders have been coming into Lanyard, at Ryan's call. It's his army he has gathered – an army of gun fighters, men who kill for pay.'

Trumbull placed his head between his hands. 'I have learned to accept this country according to its own standards. I have made it my own land. I find it within myself to fight for what I believe is right, even if it is necessary to kill. But before I make a final decision, I'd like to talk with Billy Bascom.'

Pete Burnett shook his head. 'Men like us talk over things before we do them. That's not Billy's way. He rode out an hour ago. If you'd seen his face, you wouldn't have tried to stop him. He didn't say where he was going, but it's my guess he wants to talk to Vaughn Morgan.'

Trumbull lifted his head. 'Billy will kill him?'

Burnett shrugged. 'Morgan would be luckier if Billy did. I told the kid you'd need evidence before you'd act. Your way is the right way as far as he is concerned. He'll make Morgan talk. If he's the stubborn type, he won't be pretty to look at, but he'll spill his guts before Billy's through with him.'

Trumbull was pale, but his lean face was set in determined lines. 'Then the most we can do is wait.'

Swenson moved impatiently. 'Wait, hell! I'm passing the word to San Antonio, El Paso, Dodge and the rest of the hell towns that Trumbull and Swenson are in the market for fast guns. I just hope to God, Ryan will give us time to get some of them here.' He crossed to the door, paused there. 'In the meantime, listen to Pete here – and Billy if he gets back. They'll keep you alive.'

The door slammed behind him. Pete Burnett remained in front of the desk. 'Killing isn't my idea of fun any more than it's yours. I've walked around trouble so long, trying not to learn to like it, when it has to be faced I feel a little sick. Just the same the time has come when it can't be avoided.'

Trumbull nodded, soberly. 'I keep thinking how much harder it is for Billy. This will end his last chance to be something other than what he has always been. I have a queer feeling about Billy – what you would call a hunch. Men like Ryan feel themselves touched by destiny, but it is men like Billy who will be remembered.'

In the silence of the room the muffled thump of Swenson's horse riding out sounded like distant thunder.

Conchita Noriega dipped her little finger into the tiny jar and carefully outlined her full lips with bright red rouge. By the light of the two lamps, one to either side of her streaked mirror, she sat, lost in thought, her dark eyes half closed. They opened abruptly as a knock sounded at her door, and a frown marred the straight line of her brows.

'I'll be there in a momento, Enrique!' she called, impatiently.

A man's deep voice answered her. 'It ain't Enrique, it's me, Bob. I got news for you, baby.'

Conchita's frown deepened. 'The only news you would carry would be bad, hombre,' she returned. 'Go away. You will see me when I dance. I will let you buy me a drink.'

'Maybe I'll be buyin' you a hell of a lot more than that,' Oringer said, quickly. 'That interest you, baby?'

For a moment, Conchita remained still, then she stood up in her quick supple way, crossed to the door and drew it open. Bob Oringer's heavy figure stepped into the room.

'That's more like it,' he said, grinning. 'You're goin' to find out I can pay for what I want, Conchita – with hard money, not sweet words that buy you nothin'. You see this star on my vest? I'm deputy sheriff of Lanyard County. That's the first step up for me. Ryan's goin' to win this country, an' he's goin' to find it hard to do without me.' He stopped. 'You know how I feel about you, an' you don't give a damn. But that's goin' to change. You like to dress up fancy. You spend every dime you get your hands on for junk jewellery and shiny clothes. How'd you like to be a real lady, Conchita, with money to pay for every damn thing you ever wanted in your life?'

For a moment she stared at him, then tossed her head and laughed. 'And you will buy these things for me? Stop drinking *pulque*. It's making you loco.'

He shook his head, slowly. 'Go ahead, laugh,' he said. 'But I know you, baby! You're not stupid, you can figger things out for yourself. The higher Ryan climbs, the more he's going to need my help, an' the more it's goin' to cost him.' His eyes met hers and held them. 'You ever think about other places, Conchita – big towns, and fancy people, and stores it'll take you a week to buy your way through?'

The girl's eyes half closed. Dreams were a trap for fools who believed in them, but Oringer, she knew, was no fool.

'What would you give to have it like that?' he whispered, hoarsely.

Her eyes met his boldly. 'Everything!' she answered, but drew back when he reached for her. Her face was all Apache in that instant. 'Talk is wind, and so are promises,' she said.

Oringer kept grinning. He had changed, she thought; he was more sure of himself, and of her.

'Take your time,' he said. 'I can wait.' He reached behind him for the door, opened it, and backed out. 'You want to be shown, it won't take me long, I promise you that!'

Conchita closed the door, then turned and walked back to the mirror. She had lost most of her illusions along with her virginity when Enrique had caught her alone in the house when she was thirteen. She knew what she meant to most men, and the knowledge neither shamed nor frightened her. She had seen what happened to other half-breed girls, had seen the change that so few years could bring. And it frightened her more than anything, even the thought of dying. For so long as she could see in her mirror what she saw now, what every man she met saw and desired, her dreams remained possible. But every day, every week, every month, made them further away from reality.

She stared at her reflection in the mirror, and saw the hard, new lines about her mouth and eyes. She thought about Bob Oringer, and what he had promised – and she thought about Billy Bascom, too. Sweet words that buy you nothing …

*

Vaughn Morgan sat uneasily on the spring seat of the buckboard. He kept swinging his head, watching the horizon, until the horseman to his left leaned in to speak.

'What's eatin' you, Morgan? Got the spooks?' Paul Dorman's brown face grinned at him. 'You think Billy Bascom's got you marked for his fifteenth notch?'

'I don't think nothin'!' Morgan retorted angrily.

Jerry Lanham, who rode on the far side, one leg crooked about the horn of his saddle, winked at Dorman. 'That's why Ryan sent us with you. Triangle takes care of its own, even bastards like you.'

Morgan glared at him. 'You talk big,' he said. 'You was there when Pete Burnett made the old man back water. I didn't see you rilin' up none.'

Lanham shrugged. 'Ryan's the tall man. I get paid for doin' what he says. Like now. We're doin' you a favour. The old man says cut out fifty head an' road-brand 'em an' run 'em into Fort Messina. Just to get you out of the way in case any of your Horn friends decide to pay their respects to you with a hunk of lead. I wouldn't give a wet poop if Billy Bascom cut your heart out, but I do what I'm told, even wet-nursin' you.'

'Do me no favours,' Morgan returned, sullenly.

Lanham winked at Dorman again. 'Me, I've had my run-in with the kid. An' I've slept with one eye open ever since. I keep thinkin' about that greaser he killed sometime back. The Mex had his gun in his hand before the kid dropped him with a slug in one eye. Somebody asked him, real polite-like, "Hey, Billy, what number does this make?" An' Bascom, hummin' that loco song under his breath like he always does, says, "I don't count Indians an' Mexicans." Hey, Morgan, you think he'd count a yellow-belly like you?'

Dorman's harsh, braying laughter rang out.

'Goddamn it!' Morgan yelled. 'Leave me alone!'

'Anythin' to oblige you,' Dorman said, grinning crookedly. 'Pull up here. You get a fire goin', get the iron hot. Me an' Jerry'll rustle up the cows.'

Morgan's anger died. Being left alone was the last thing he

60

wanted just now. He still remembered the scream of a Horn man as he died beneath the hoofs of the stampede – just as he remembered the terrifying instant when he had ridden back to make sure the stampede had done its work and had seen Billy Bascom riding away, unharmed. Billy had seen Morgan leaving the camp in the middle of the night, and he would not forget. Some of the stories he had heard about Billy Bascom's ideas of vengeance burned holes in Morgan's memory.

For an instant he started to ask one of them to stay with him, then he read the contempt in their eyes and angrily pulled in the team and kicked on the brakes.

'All right, damn it, stop gabbin' an' get it done. I'll build your lousy fire.' Morgan watched them go, and involuntarily swept the horizon with his eyes. He followed them until they were lost to sight, and again glanced around. From the buckboard he had a clear view for some distance, and it would shorten when he climbed down. But if he hadn't built the branding fire and heated the iron by the time Lanham and Dorman came back, they'd make his life a hell of contemptuous ridicule.

He swung down from the buckboard, walked to the back of the rig and hauled out the firewood. He carried it away from the wagon some distance and bent to the task of making the fire. It was plain enough, he thought, sullenly, that he couldn't stay on Triangle. Lanham and Dorman would see to that, and that crazy kid, Billy Bascom, would remain a more serious threat. Morgan's mouth curved downward. To hell with them all! There wasn't a thing to stop him from riding on when they reached Messina. There were better places than Lanyard County. Maybe he'd drift west into Arizona for a spell. There was that bed-crazy squaw in Nogales....

Busy with his own thoughts, Morgan built a glowing bed of coals and laid the road-brand iron across them. He straightened at last, and still building pictures in his mind, walked toward the buckboard. He had almost reached it before he became aware of the slim man who stood there, a rifle cradled in his arms.

'Hello, Vaughn,' Billy Bascom said, gently. His half-smile

revealed his bold upper teeth. 'You're a hard man to get close to, but here we are. Now we're goin' to talk.'

CHAPTER 6

Shocked surprise held Vaughn Morgan rigid for an instant, then his eyes narrowed. 'You may be crazy, kid, but not crazy enough to fire that rifle.'

Billy's smile remained lazily in place. 'If Lanham an' Dorman heard a shot, they'd circle in slow, too slow to do you any good, Vaughn.'

Morgan's feeling of utter desperation began to crumble into a strange, new excitement. He had never felt this way before. He had spent hours working with a revolver and held himself to be as fast as the next man, but until this moment he had sensed a subtle difference; a gun fighter had no self-doubt, no nerves to fight under control. Morgan had never been able to realize that sense of detachment, of supreme self-confidence. Always before his own fears had prevented him from a final showdown. There was always an out, even if he had to run for it. But now there was none.

He studied the kid's face, his casual stance, the looseness of his grip on the rifle. Billy held it in what seemed an awkward manner, his left hand on the stock. A right-handed man always held an advantage over a southpaw. These thoughts came unbidden into Morgan's mind. He licked his lips. The man who killed Billy Bascom would inherit the kid's rep, and that was something Vaughn Morgan prized almost as highly as his life. If he killed the kid, men like Lanham and Dorman would lose their contempt, and the thought burned away Morgan's fear.

The rifle lowered an inch as the kid's arms relaxed. A singing tension rang through Vaughn Morgan's mind, and he felt the buzzing roar of blood in his ears. If the rifle dropped a half-inch lower ...

Billy moved, and the rifle sagged, almost as if in response to Morgan's thoughts. Instantly Morgan's right hand shot in and up, dragging at his holstered Colt. Even as he made his move, he heard the kid's triumphant laugh, saw his slender figure start with blinding speed directly toward him. Morgan sagged down and back, desperately, fighting to get his gun level. He saw the kid's shoulders bunch then the rifle was a blurred streak, ramming at his head. He tried to twist away, and the smash of the rifle against his head was a titanic explosion, and the world broke apart....

Billy felt the impact of the rifle against Morgan's head, and stepped back. He saw Morgan fall, and cursed himself for having struck too hard. He dropped the gun and knelt to probe at Morgan's throat, then slowly his smile returned. The other man was still breathing. For a moment Billy stared down into the dust-covered face, then spat to one side. Burnett had made it clear that Morgan dead meant nothing at all; he had to be made to talk.

Billy studied the horizon. To the east, a mile or so away, was a building cloud of dust. That would be the two Triangle riders with the herd. That gave him damn little time, and taking Morgan with him was out of the question now. The mare wouldn't carry double, and the buckboard team wouldn't stand a chance against the two riders. Billy frowned, then his eyes took in the branding fire, the road-brand iron thrust into the red coals. He bent, caught Morgan under the arms and dragged him toward the fire. He looked once more at the oncoming herd, then picked up the branding iron....

The banjo clock on the fly-specked, adobe wall of the sheriff's office ticked loudly in the hot silence of the room. Jem Mace eased his swivel chair back, hawked noisily, then spat toward a filthy spittoon at one side of his desk. Dirty, circular spots marked his misses, and he did no better this time. He wiped his drooping, yellow moustache with the back of one scrawny hand then looked up at his visitors.

'It's somethin' to think about,' he said almost grudgingly.

Nils Swenson's sandy brows knitted together. 'Think, hell!' he snapped.

'Don't pay a man to get riled up in this heat, Swenson,' Jem Mace said, mildly. 'This ain't the first time I've worn a star, an' I learned early in the game to jump slow and sure.'

'Or not at all!' Swenson cut in, bitterly. He swung around to face Trumbull. 'I told you comin' here was a waste of time!'

The Englishman's sober expression didn't change. 'I wanted to see for myself.'

Something in his voice and manner made Mace frown for the first time. 'Now look here,' he blustered. 'I don't like that kind of talk. You an' Swenson are important men in this county, but so's Jason Ryan.' His talon-like hand rapped on the piece of paper atop his desk. 'But who's Vaughn Morgan? A two-bit saddle-thumper nobody gives a damn about. Maybe he's carryin' a grudge against Ryan; maybe he's just shootin' his mouth off. Most likely that wild Indian, Billy Bascom, gun-whipped him into signin' this here thing.'

Trumbull smiled coldly. He bent and picked up the paper, folded it and tucked it into a pocket. He saw the sudden alarm in Mace's eyes. 'You'll find, Mr Mace,' he said, quietly, 'no matter how high your authority goes, there's always someone above you. I think this might apply equally well to Governor Carlisle. At least I intend to find out.'

Mace straightened so suddenly his chair springs squealed. 'Just a minute,' he blustered. 'You come in here with a serious charge – that paper's evidence I ought to keep.'

'What charge, Sheriff?' Trumbull's smile remained without humour. 'You didn't seem to think there was one.'

Swenson turned and strode angrily toward the stairs that led down to the street. After another look at Mace, Trumbull followed. The sheriff watched them go, his eyes narrowed with worried thought. He spat again and wiped at his mouth. For a moment he sat still, thinking hard, then he got to his feet, lifted his hat from the rack and hurried downstairs.

On the street, he marked Trumbull and Swenson moving away, then spun about and hurried toward the livery stables where he kept his horse.

*

The plate glass window that filled one wall of Jason Ryan's adobe-walled living room had been made to order from the biggest store in El Paso, and it had cost Ryan a small fortune to acquire. Woven Indian drapes that hung to either side made a gaudy splash of colour against the whitewashed adobe bricks. The Spanish tiles on the floor had been shipped by mule train from Mexico City, and only a few public buildings could boast its equal. Like the man who had built it, the room was big and florid and without warmth.

Jason Ryan stood before the big window now, staring out across the rolling grasslands to the far hills that marked the boundary of his domain. Behind him, Jem Mace shuffled his booted feet nervously.

'I saw the damned thing, Jason,' he said, stridently. 'I don't like it. There could be trouble.'

Ryan turned slowly. 'I don't expect this to be fun.' His carved rock face swung toward Bob Oringer, who lounged against one side of the empty fireplace. 'Have you kept Morgan out of sight?'

Oringer nodded. 'Lanham an' Dorman found him where they'd left him. That damn Bascom must have come at him like a cat. Morgan was still screamin' his guts out.' He grinned suddenly. 'Billy used a branding iron on him – marked him like a maverick. Lanham hauled him to the old line cabin on Mule Back Ridge while Dorman rode in with the news.'

Ryan nodded. He swung back to the window. 'Mace, I want a warrant sworn out for the arrest of Trumbull, Burnett and Bascom.'

Jem Mace's horse-like face registered surprise. 'You goin' to charge them with workin' over Morgan? Hell, Jason ...'

Without turning around, Ryan cut in. 'I told you this wasn't going to be pretty. You'll charge them with the murder of Vaughn Morgan. Them you'll take Oringer and swear in as many men as you'll need and ride into Horn.'

'Hell, Jason, are you crazy? Morgan ain't ...'

'Vaughn Morgan is dead,' Ryan interrupted, coldly. He turned to face Bob Oringer. 'Billy Bascom used the hot iron on Morgan to make him talk, then shot him in the back of the head to finish the

65

job. Lanham and Dorman saw the whole thing – didn't they, Bob?'

Oringer's ugly smile flickered into place. 'That's the way it was.'

Ryan held motionless for a moment. 'Trumbull is a stubborn man. He'll be belligerent when he's arrested. Before that happens, Bob, you'll burn that forged paper Trumbull and Swenson showed Mace, and you'll get Trumbull's signature on a blank piece of paper. Do you understand me?'

Oringer's right hand moved to his holstered Colt; eased its weight in the leather. 'Sure, Jason.' Oringer grinned. 'First I'll bring in poor Morgan's dead body.' He swung around, his high heels rapped sharply against the tile floor. He closed the heavy oak door behind him.

Jason Ryan had already turned back to the big window and was staring out across his land.

It was the time of evening that Harry Trumbull enjoyed most, when the last tip of the blazing sun had canted behind the distant Torollones, and the mad colours of a spilled paint-box streaked the sky. His eyes were clouded with thought as he stared out at the darkening plain.

He was alone, against Pete Burnett's judgment and protests, but the complete feeling of being alone was still new enough for Trumbull to enjoy it. This was one of those times, for the decision to fight back was behind him, and he could relax for this brief while to enjoy to the fullest this fierce, new sense of independence he had come to know.

A rumble of hoofs stirred him. It would be Burnett and Billy, and the two remaining riders of Horn, coming in from the range. Their orders had been to drive back the Triangle cattle, and to salvage what they could from the line camp. The room was dark with shadows, and Trumbull stood up to light the hanging lamp. Hoofs drummed into the yard, and a moment later boots clattered on the broad front porch. A door slammed, and Trumbull frowned.

'That you, Pete?' he called out.

The sudden yellow flood of light from the lamp blinded him for an instant, and he blinked. There was no reply to his call, and for the first time he felt alarm. He had started toward his desk and the holstered revolver that hung beside it, when the door slammed open and a man stepped into the room. He held a drawn Colt in his hand, and his ugly face was smiling.

'Hold it, Trumbull!' he ordered.

'What's the meaning of this?' the Englishman demanded, angrily.

The other man ignored him. 'It's all right, Mace. Trumbull's here an' he's alone.'

Jem Mace came into the room frowning, and a third man followed him. Somewhere in the house a door banged and a man's voice yelled out, 'The place is empty. Nothin' stirrin'.'

Trumbull recognized the man holding the Colt as Bob Oringer. The Triangle man's grin widened. 'OK, Jerry, stay outside an' keep your eyes open.'

Still ignoring Trumbull, Oringer surveyed the room, then moved toward the paper-littered desk. He bent over it scanning papers, then throwing them to the floor impatiently. His movements were hurried, and it was obvious he knew what he wanted.

'You can't do that!' Trumbull grasped Oringer's thickly muscled arm, and then was slammed back as the bigger man jerked about. Oringer's left hand doubled into a fist and smashed into Trumbull's face. The Englishman staggered under the force of the blow and tried to strike back, but Oringer was stronger, faster. The deputy's right hand struck hard, swinging the barrel of his Colt against the side of Trumbull's head. The smaller man fell heavily, half-unconscious. Oringer turned back to the desk, began to rummage through the drawers.

Trumbull forced his trembling arms to lift him to a sitting position, his mouth was bleeding, staining his shirt front.

Oringer threw him a glance over one wide shoulder. He grinned maliciously. 'You're under arrest, Trumbull, for the murder of Vaughn Morgan. Your gunslinger Bascom did the job, but you ordered it done. An' that makes you guilty as all hell.' The grin twisted awry, and Oringer picked up a pen and a blank sheet of paper, moved to stand over Trumbull where he sat on the floor.

'We'll start by getting' your John Henry on this piece of paper.' He dropped the paper and pen in front of Trumbull. 'You're goin' to sign it, whether you want to or not – but I want you to say no. I want you to keep on sayin' it, because there ain't nothin' I'd enjoy more than seein' just how much of a beatin' a skinny bastard like you can take.'

Trumbull stared into the ugly, sweating face peering down at him, then looked at Jem Mace. The sheriff was watching them, his face pale and blank.

'Are you insane?' Trumbull started to get up. Oringer reached down with his left hand, grabbed Trumbull's long, sandy-coloured hair in a painful grip, then chopped down with his right hand with all the strength of his ox-like shoulders behind the blow. Trumbull heard the meaty sound of the blow, felt his shoulder and neck go numb, and then blackness closed over his mind....

He came to, writhing with pain, hearing a scream that he knew had come from his own lips. He fought it back. His head and shoulders were sheer agony, and his left hand was bloody and bruised from where the high heels of Oringer's boots had torn flesh and cartilage. Oringer was bent over, watching him, his ugly face beaded with sweat.

'Just keep on sayin' no,' he whispered. 'I got all the time there is.'

Trumbull shook his head. 'No more, please,' he answered, brokenly. 'My God, aren't you human? Isn't there any decency in you?'

Oringer's reply was to bend his leg and drive the pointed toe of his boot into Trumbull's groin. The Englishman screamed again, doubled over and vomited. 'I'll sign it,' he gasped. 'Anything!'

A pen was thrust into his right hand, guided to paper he couldn't see. He scrawled his name. The scratching of the pen nib was loud in the silence of the room. Oringer jerked the paper away, looked at it, then stuffed it into a shirt pocket. Trumbull's eyes rolled up into his head, and he fell back unconscious.

'Goddamn it, Bob!' Mace cursed, angrily. 'He's out for good this time, an' we still haven't found that paper Morgan signed.'

Oringer frowned. 'No, we ain't,' he agreed, slowly. Then his face changed, and a sly expression filled it. 'But there's more than one way of spinnin' a hog. Ryan said to burn it. We'll just do that little thing.'

He reached up, lifted the hanging lamp from its brackets. He balanced there in the centre of the room, then threw the lamp to smash against the wooden desk. The glass shade exploded, and coal oil spilled over the paper-littered floor. The flame of the wick caught with a dull boom, and fire spread hungrily, began to crackle. Some eddied up, and thickened.

'Damn it to hell!' Jem Mace shouted.

'Get goin'. We're through here,' Oringer ordered.

'What about Bascom an' Burnett?'

'Get 'em later,' Oringer said, and moved toward the door. Reddish light grew brighter, and the wallpaper began to darken and burn.

'But – Trumbull –' Mace hesitated in the doorway.

'Get out!' Oringer yelled, savagely, and the sheriff moved into the hall. Bob Oringer followed him, then turned back, grinning into the flaming, smoking room. His right hand jerked down and up, and his levelled Colt barked angrily, once, twice, three times. Trumbull's prone figure jarred at the impact of the shots. Oringer swung away. He saw Mace staring at him.

'Tryin' to escape, wasn't he, Sheriff?' The Colt was still naked in Oringer's fist. The sheriff nodded hurriedly; Oringer holstered his gun. 'It's a good thing for you to remember, Jem,' he said.

They hurried down the hall. Behind them the flames grew brighter, began to lick around the doorframe.

Billy Bascom first saw the red glow against the sky, and his shout drew Pete Burnett's attention. Behind Burnett, Hank Lewis yelled, 'It's the big house!'

Billy drove home his spurs, and the mare broke into a dead run. Billy stood in the stirrups, the wind whipping into his face, careless of risk, of the danger of racing a horse at night over broken ground. He came into the ranch yard and hit the ground running. The crackle of flames was a dull thunder, the red-yellow glare stood up into the sky like a flaming finger.

Billy sent a fast look about him, then raced for the porch. The roof of the house was afire, and smoky flames were eating down the uprights of the porch. A window shattered in the heat like the explosion of a rifle.

'Trumbull!' Billy's call racketed above the sullen roar of the burning building. He called again, then stared into the red-lit interior of the house. For an instant he hesitated, then, throwing his arms up before his face, he bent over and leaped up to the porch. He reached the door, smashed it open with a single kick of his booted foot, backed to avoid the hungry flames that shot out, and then plunged inside. Curtains smouldered at the windows, and the varnish was blistering on the furniture. The big living room was empty, and Billy ran down the long hall toward Trumbull's office.

It was like leaping into the maw of a roaring furnace. Billy felt his face blister, his eyebrows burn away. He jumped through the door, dodged a downfall of burning lath from the gaping ceiling. He saw a huddled form in the centre of the floor, and a low cry escaped him. He bent over it. Trumbull's clothes were beginning to char and blacken, and his hair was smouldering. Billy beat out the glowing sparks, caught the fallen man under his arms, and backed crazily for the door. Even as he gained it, the rest of the ceiling crashed down, and flames, open now to the sky, leaped higher.

Down the smoke-filled hall Billy dragged the body of Harry Trumbull. He stumbled, fell to his haunches, but got up and kept going. Then another man was beside him, helping him. Between them they carried Trumbull out of the house and into the yard, away from the heat of the burning building. Pete Burnett's solemn, fire-blackened face twisted as he bent over Trumbull. He straightened, slowly.

'He's still alive – barely,' he said. 'There are three slugs in him.'

Billy dropped to his knees, cushioned Trumbull's head on his lap. Trumbull's blistered eyelids moved, then opened, slowly. The glazed, dying eyes saw the kid's face. Recognition flickered in them.

The burned, bloody lips moved, and Billy bent closer.

'Who did it?' he demanded, hoarsely.

'Sheriff ... Oringer ... two of Ryan's ... men ...' The weak voice broke. The burned eyes closed, then opened again, staring up into the night sky. 'This is a good land ... worth fighting for ... worth ...' The charred, beaten face moved to a terrible agony. 'Worth dying for ...'

Trumbull sighed heavily, and then some inner strength seemed to flow away, and he lay still.

Pete Burnett straightened. He pulled off his hat, and turned to stare at the fiercely burning house. A side wall crashed down, and sparks shot a hundred feet into the sky.

'We'll take him into Lanyard,' Burnett said slowly. 'Swenson will want to give him a decent funeral. It'll be our last work for Horn.'

Jake Haley and Hank Lewis came up, pulling off their hats. Their faces were grim.

Billy Bascom looked up at them. His fire-blackened face was streaked on both cheeks by tears that had left white furrows. 'It won't be my last work for Trumbull,' he said, his voice barely audible. His boy's face was gaunt with hard, murderous lines. 'I've got some killin' to do.'

CHAPTER 7

In the warm, moist darkness of the room, a match flared briefly, and in its glow Billy could see the shine of Conchita's dark eyes, looking at him. She was resting on one arm, and the bare shoulders glistened in the light as if filmed with oil. 'It's almost morning,' she said softly.

'This might be the last time in a long while I can come to you,' Billy responded, softly.

'And there will be the time when you cannot come at all.' She spoke without tone. Then suddenly she was in his arms, and the

71

soft warmth of her body was against him. 'It does not have to be like this, Billy. Trumbull is gone, forget him. Ryan will need men and Oringer is too big a fool to last long. You could take his place with Ryan ...'

His hand went across her mouth, stopping the words. She brushed his hand away passionately. 'Then go away from here. Take me with you! I would work for you, love you ...'

'And be another half-breed woman married to a hobo cowhand,' he cut in, bitterly, 'It won't work, Conchita. If Ryan and Oringer would let me ride away now, it would still be a hard scrabble the rest of our lives. Trouble follows me like my shadow. You're young and pretty now, but livin' the way we'd have to would make you old in a hurry. You'd hate my guts in a year.'

'Do you think it would be any easier for me here, Billy?' she demanded. 'Now a dance and song is enough, and they come back to see me. But it won't be long before my dancing and singing won't be enough. And how long does it take a half-breed whore to go to hell?'

'It won't happen to you,' Billy answered, gravely. 'You're like a cat; you'll always land on your feet.'

He felt her body tremble in his arms. 'Billy, don't you know what it's like to be a half-breed girl? I'm nothing, just a plaything for gringo men. Do they lift their hats when they pass me on the street, like they do for white women? Do they care if I hear their filthy talk? No, because I'm just an animal, without feelings. But inside, Billy, I'm like other women, white women. I want to be like them, have the things they have, know that I'm something more than just brown trash.'

Billy kissed her, gently, 'I promise you, *amada*, you'll wear silk and rustle when you walk like the finest lady you ever saw.' He bent, kissed her again. 'About this we'll talk another time. Now I must go.'

He swung his legs from the bed and stood up.

'Billy, wait ...' She heard his light footsteps cross the floor, then the scrape of his boots as he slipped easily through the high window. His feet thudded softly to the ground outside, then silence

72

filled the room. For a moment Conchita sat very still, then her eyes closed, and bitter tears welled from under her lids.

The black hearse wheeled down the dusty street of Lanyard, and the few flowers that topped the plain pine casket were wilted by the noonday heat. The dust, lifted by the walking hoofs of the horses, rose above the heads of the riders who flanked the black carriage. They rode as a silent, armed group, dressed in their Sunday best, but each man wore his revolver at his hip and carried a rifle cradled in his arms. Their eyes were alert and watchful, and the silent villagers, who were not a part of the struggle beginning to shape up in Lanyard County, watched with worried frowns.

Billy rode to the right of the hearse, beside Pete Burnett. He could see Nils Swenson's huge shape on the far side. Swenson rode heavily, without grace, and his sun-reddened face was set with sullen anger. Juan, the Horn cook, had disappeared, wanting no part of what was happening, and the remaining Horn riders kept together. Opposite them, and behind the carriage, rode Swenson and his seven men. Billy knew one or two of them by sight, and more than one of the others by reputation. Swenson had wasted no time hiring guns, and the men he had picked out were branded by the marks of their trade, from their curiously bland faces to the careless arrogance of their manners.

Billy caught Burnett's eye, saw that the Horn ramrod had been looking at Swenson and his men. There was a deep worry in Burnett's eyes, and a thoughtful frown on his face. Billy thought, he's tryin to make up his mind which way to jump, but there's nothing for him to decide about. He made up his mind a long time ago.

The funeral procession filed through the single narrow street of the town, and beyond it swung up the rise toward the graveyard on the hill above the town. The cemetery had once been fenced, but now the wire strands were broken, and the posts sagged wearily. Many of the wooden grave markers had fallen, and most of the graves had sunk below the level of the surrounding ground, rect-angular pocks in the brown-grass face of the slope. They passed a

73

few iron-fenced pots where flowers grew, cared for by patient-eyed Mexicans who carried water each day up the hill. Just ahead a raw, ugly mound of yellow earth was piled, and the dark maw of an open grave stood out. A long-faced Mexican leaned against the handle of a shovel thrust into the mound of dry earth, waiting for them. His eyes were closed, and his face wore a harsh, beaten look.

The hearse stopped beside the grave, and the black-clad preacher climbed down. His manner was nervous, and his eyes kept staring at the rifles of the armed men who surrounded him.

Nils Swenson dismounted with a grunt. The angry look remained stamped indelibly on his red face. Billy climbed down, and he and Pete Burnett walked together to the hearse. They slid out the coffin, and the other Horn riders moved silently up to grasp the iron handles. Swenson's crew remained in the saddle, looking back toward the town, their faces expressionless, their eyes narrowed and wary.

The men of Horn carried the coffin to the canvas sling that would lower it into the grave when the undertaker turned a crank. They backed away and removed their hats. Billy felt the heat of the sun pressing down upon his bare head.

The minister cleared his throat nervously, then stepped forward. He spoke quickly in a blurred mumble of sound. He finished, mopped his face with a red bandana, and then lustily blew his nose. He moved back to the hearse and seemed anxious to be gone.

The undertaker removed the few flowers, piling them to one side, then began to crank the casket down into the grave. The winch squeaked and groaned, and the black box slowly sank into the earth. It struck the bottom of the hole, and the undertaker unfastened the sling, drew it out. He nodded toward the Mexican, and the man bent slowly, lifted a full shovel of dirt and listlessly dropped it into the grave.

Nils Swenson pulled on his hat. 'Come back to the store,' he said, gruffly. 'I've got some plain talkin' to do.' He returned to his horse, climbed heavily to the saddle and rode back down the hill, his sharp-eyed riders falling in behind him.

Billy moved over to stand at the edge of the grave. Pete Burnett came up beside him. They stood there in silence, each framing the words of goodbye they would not speak aloud, and then Burnett turned away. He walked a few paces to his horse, then swung back.

'Comin', Billy?'

'In a minute,' Billy replied.

The Mexican labourer worked slowly and steadily in the heat. Billy heard the clip-clop of hoofs, glanced up to see Burnett and the other two Horn men returning to the town.

He stood there in silence while the grave was filled, the last of the loose earth heaped and rounded. The Mexican listlessly shaped the mound, patted it, then shouldered the shovel and moved away. The black-clad mortician came up silently and arranged the wilted flowers atop the grave, then returned to the hearse and drove it back down the hill.

A vagrant breeze spun a dust whorl over the weathered face of the cemetery; Billy looked across the squalid graveyard toward the limitless sweep of the grasslands beyond. For a moment he remained there, silently, then he said, 'Goodbye, Mr Trumbull,' softly, then replaced his hat and walked back to his horse. He rode down the hill without looking back.

Swenson's store was in a big, clapboard warehouse set behind a high, adobe wall that had once fronted a magnificent adobe ranch house long since destroyed by fire. All that remained of the original building was a square, single-storey wing that adjoined the warehouse. A low veranda ran across the face of the adobe structure, with a hitch rail before it. A dozen horses were tied here, and as Billy rode the mare through the open gateway in the adobe wall, he saw a man with a rifle leaning there on guard.

Billy dismounted, looped the reins over the hitch rail, then moved into the shade of the veranda roof. Pete Burnett sat on the hitch rail, long legs dangling. He was smoking a cigarette, his face expressionless. Nils Swenson was pacing angrily up and down, his boot heels clumping on the wooden floor. Jake Haley and Hank Lewis leaned against the adobe wall, watching the other two men expressionlessly.

Swenson swung about as Billy came onto the porch. 'Maybe you can talk some sense into his damn fool head!' he rapped out. He gestured irately toward Burnett. 'He's either crazy, or yellow.'

'You've got enough enemies now,' Billy cut in. 'You say somethin' like that again, an' you can count me as another.'

Swenson stared at him, then shook his head. 'All right, damn it, I'm sorry. I know Pete Burnett's as good a man as I've ever met – and the stubbornest goddamn mule that ever walked.'

Burnett was looking straight ahead. Billy faced him. 'What's the joke, Pete?'

'No joke, kid,' Burnett replied. 'A man rides the way that suits him best. I'm not ridin' Swenson's.'

'Be sensible, Pete!' Swenson butted in. 'Look, I'll make it plain. Jem Mace an' his deputy, Bob Oringer, an' two of Ryan's men – Jerry Lanham an' Paul Dorman, you know them both – had a warrant for Trumbull's arrest. There were two other names on that warrant, Billy Bascom's an' yours.'

Burnett nodded. 'A man who rakes in a full pot doesn't stoop after coppers that fall on the floor. Once you've lost your stake, what difference does it make if you figger you've been cheated? The stake's gone. You get another one.'

'And let Ryan get away with what he's done?'

Burnett flipped his cigarette away and looked steadily into Swenson's angry face. 'You tell me how I can stop him from gettin' away with it, an' I'll go along with you.' His long face moved into harsh lines. 'Do you think I liked buryin' the whitest man I ever met? But there are lots of things I don't like, and not one of them is worth dyin' for. That's what you'll be doin', you an' you an' every gun you can buy. You've got a dozen men, but Ryan's got a hundred. He'll stomp you into the ground.'

Swenson held very still, then shook his head savagely. 'A man rides high only so long, Pete. Then somebody takes a fall out of him. This mornin' Ryan presented a note to the bank, claimin' it was a lien against Horn. It wouldn't fool a blind man. Me an' Trumbull was partners. I own a half interest. You damned well know Trumbull wouldn't borrow money from Ryan, an' if he did, he wouldn't put up something he didn't own as guarantee. I don't know how Ryan got that note signed, an' I don't give a damn. I'm going' to grab first. We're takin' over Horn this afternoon. I'll stop Ryan one way or another.'

'You'll try,' Burnett said, quietly. 'But that's what Ryan wants you to do. He's got all the high cards now.' His face set in a hard mask. 'He'll lose them, sooner or later, an' when he does, I'll be waitin' – with the kind of law men like Ryan can't buy. If you're smart, you'll wait, too.' Burnett slid down from the hitch rail, stood straight and tall. 'But you won't, any more than Billy will. I'll bury you both.'

He turned and walked around the rail, untied his horse, swung up into the saddle and, without looking back, rode out.

Swenson cursed viciously for a moment, then faced Billy. 'How about you, kid? And Haley and Lewis?'

Billy stared after Pete Burnett's lanky figure for a moment, then nodded. 'Count me in,' he said.

Hank Lewis said, quietly: 'That goes for me an' Jake, too.'

'All right, then!' Swenson ordered. 'Get your gear. We're ridin' for Horn now!'

They rode out of Lanyard, a heavily armed group of eleven men. Nils Swenson was in the lead, and Billy Bascom rode beside him. Like the others, Billy had changed into his working clothes, and he was strangely aware of the weight of his Colt revolver where it sagged over his left hip, butt foremost.

He had spent an hour that morning, working with his gun. Fine oil was still ingrained in the palms of his hands despite the sand he had rubbed into them to remove it. His left forearm was sore from enforced practice with the weapon, but the long weeks he had gone without his side arm had not noticeably slowed his draw. For a moment, when he had buckled the cartridge belt around his waist, he had felt sharp regret, and an odd sense of losing something he would never find again, but he had shrugged it away.

Long shadows rode before them by the time they reached the gate to Horn. Three men stood there, waiting for them, their horses to one side. Swenson pulled up and swivelled his head to study the open land about them. The three men were alone.

'Jem Mace an' two of his deputies,' Jake Haley said, frowning.

Swenson walked his horse forward, his broad back stiff and erect, his manner wary. Haley and Lewis both looked toward Billy as he followed Swenson down the rutted road.

Jem Mace's pole-thin shape loomed tall. He had his black Stetson pushed back from his face, and he held up his right hand officiously. Swenson rode close before reining in. He considered Mace and the two deputies sullenly.

Mace stepped forward. 'It's no good comin' out here, Nils,' the sheriff said. 'There's a lien filed on this property ...'

'Take it up with Trumbull's heirs,' Swenson answered shortly. 'Title to this land is held jointly by Trumbull an' me. There ain't no lien on my half. I'm taking over to protect my own interest.'

Mace's horsey face held a worried expression as he glanced toward his two men.

Swenson eased his weight in the saddle. 'Now, if you ain't got any other business here, get out of my way.' Swenson dropped his right hand to the butt of his holstered Colt and waited.

It was dumped into Jem Mace's lap, and he didn't like it. His long face moved restlessly and he wiped his mouth with the back of his hand. 'Now look, Nils, you don't want no trouble with the law, an'...'

'What law?' Swenson spat to the ground at Mace's boots. 'The kind you an' Oringer used against Trumbull?' The smouldering rage inside Swenson broke suddenly into open flame, and his voice rose to a screaming shout. 'Get off my land, you dirty, muck-eating bastard!'

He drove his spurs viciously into the flanks of his horse, and the animal lunged forward. Mace jumped frantically out of the way, banged into a fence post and held there while Swenson and his men rode past. When Billy looked back, the sheriff and his two men were mounted and riding back on the road to Lanyard.

'That tears it,' Hank Lewis declared, dryly.

Jake Haley grinned crookedly. 'No more than it was before. Yellow dogs always run with their tails between their legs, an' Mace looks right natural.' He looked at Billy, 'Kid, you figger we got the chance of a snowball in hell?'

Billy shook his head, and Jake laughed humorously. 'That's about what I figgered,' he said. 'Do me a favour, Billy. When you kill Mace, gut him for me!'

Jason Ryan's rocklike face didn't change as Jem Mace told his story. The colourful Mexican drapes were drawn across the huge window, and the hanging lamps threw yellow light on the polished tile floor. Ryan sat behind his broad desk and heard Mace through, then nodded slowly.

'All right,' he said.

Mace pulled at his tarnished, yellow moustache nervously. 'Hell, Jason, I couldn't tackle Swenson an' a dozen of his men. That damned Swede was achin' for a fight.'

'I said it was all right,' Ryan cut in. His heavy lids half closed. Across the big room, Bob Oringer sprawled at ease in a leather armchair, his booted legs thrust straight out, the star on his open vest shining in the light. 'Bob, you'll tell Mason to start shifting cattle past Three Waters. If you find any Horn cows, leave them alone. Let the herds mix. They'll all carry Triangle brands before long.'

'That'll split Horn in half,' Mace said in a troubled tone.

Ryan looked sharply toward him. 'I said you'd earn your pay, and you will! Swenson will settle in slowly. Keep him away from Three Waters, even if you have to fight. Judge Mowery will rule on the lien before Swenson can do anything to stop it. By the time Swenson wakes up to the fact he's lost half of Horn, he'll be so crazy mad he'll start a shooting war. You'll bear witness I did nothing that wasn't legal.'

Mace hesitated a moment before he nodded.

Ryan switched his gaze back to the lounging Oringer. 'You'll tell Mason I want the men kept in groups of eight or ten – and don't scatter them too far apart. It's a standing order that they are to shoot to kill any Horn rider who crosses a line north from Three Waters to the brakes.'

Oringer stood up.

'One more thing,' Ryan added. 'I'll pay a bounty of one hundred dollars for every Swenson rider they kill. Five hundred for Swenson himself, and twice that for Billy Bascom.'

Mace stared at Ryan. 'Hell, Jason, you're joking?'

Oringer waited.

The rock of Ryan's face remained cold and hard, gaze flicking to Oringer. 'You heard me, Bob. I meant every word I said.'

CHAPTER 8

Pete Burnett hoisted the last totesack into the bed of the wagon, lifted the tailgate and dropped the pins into place to lock it up. He studied the supplies he had bought and tried to remember if he had forgotten anything. The hell of it was he would no more than get out to his shack before he would remember something he had forgotten to buy. Shells for his Winchester and Colt; flour and sugar and slabs of fat salt pork, and sacks of beans; three boxes of canned goods, including milk and fruit for special occasions; a new coffee grinder and a gunny sack of dark-roasted coffee beans; kegs of nails, hammer, ax, saw, lengths of stovepipe. He frowned and shook his head. The wagonload of goods, plus the team and wagon he had bought secondhand, represented most of his savings during the three years he had worked for Harry Trumbull.

He was still aware of a faint doubt that he had made the right decision. Yet, despite the fact that Nils Swenson had remained the last three weeks on Horn without trouble beyond a few long-range skirmishes, Burnett believed he was right in what he was doing. He had never respected any man more than he had Trumbull – and he would never forget what Ryan had done. Though the time of reckoning might be vague, Burnett was certain it would come. When it did, he would settle accounts the same honest way Trumbull would have chosen. In the meantime, there was the small ranch beyond the Torollones he had owned for five years and had always planned to develop.

The thud of many hoofs interrupted his thoughts and he turned to look down the street. The frown on his face grew deeper. Jason Ryan and his Triangle crew rode the length of Lanyard like a conquering army, Ryan in the lead, his men three abreast behind him. Four others, two to each side of the street, rode ahead, eyes sharp. Burnett's wide mouth tightened into a grim line.

They passed where he stood beyond the low adobe wall fronting Swenson's store and drew up before the high-fronted Ryan-Dolan General Store down the street. A man with a rifle moved up each side of the loading platform that bellied the building and leaned against the corner. The others waited for Ryan to dismount, and, when he did, took their time following suit. Half of them moved down the street, and Burnett heard their rough laughter as they pushed into the Prairie Rose Saloon. The rest lined up in front of the Ryan-Dolan store, taking their ease against the loading dock. Like an army in a hostile town, Burnett thought.

Ryan had not spared him a single glance as he rode past, but Burnett knew he had been marked. He rubbed a hand thoughtfully against the lean hardness of his jaw. Most of the Triangle riders knew him and were watching him, waiting to see what he would do, and their grins would change to laughter if he drove out now. For a moment he held there, then turned and walked to the gateway. He stepped into the street, and three or four of the Triangle men stiffened, watching him with narrowed eyes. A thin smile bent his lips, and he walked toward them.

As he approached the steps of the store, others straightened. Cigarettes were flipped away. Hard-faced men exchanged glances, uncertain. If there had been only three or four of them, they would have known what to do, but there were too many of them present to take alarm. A lone man facing twenty made the twenty look ridiculous, and Burnett knew it. His smile tightened.

He reached the stairs, and a man stepped free of the building to stand at the top of them. It was Jerry Lanham, his sullen face twisted.

'You goin' someplace, Burnett?'

The other Triangle riders relaxed, watching the encounter, alert but not involved. Burnett saw this and nodded. 'It's a free country,' he said.

Lanham's sullenness deepened into anger. 'You declared yourself out of this fight. Stay out.'

Burnett shook his head, stepped forward, and saw Lanham tense. The other Triangle men grinned expectantly. Then a heavy step sounded behind Lanham and Jason Ryan said, 'Let him pass, Jerry.'

The stiffness drained out of Lanham's upper body and he leaned against the building. Burnett walked up the steps. As Burnett passed Lanham, he noticed the silver star pinned to his vest, then stepped past him and followed Ryan into the store.

Ryan walked ahead of him toward the centre of the big store-room. There was no tension visible when he turned. 'I don't know a better way of getting killed than poking fun at a man like Lanham.'

'You're workin on a better way, Jason,' Burnett returned. He pulled a sack of Golden Grain from his shirt pocket, slipped free a wheat-straw paper, and rolled a cigarette. He lit it while Ryan stared coldly.

'You come here to say that?' Ryan asked.

Burnett blew out smoke and shook his head. 'No. Two other reasons. I'm not bucking you, Jason. I don't figger I have to. Give a man like you enough rope an' he'll hang himself with it. But I'm not runnin away from you, either.'

Ryan's stone-like face didn't alter. 'All right, you've said it.'

'There's more,' Burnett drew smoke into his lungs, exhaled slowly. 'I don't give a damn about what happens to you, but I want to warn you against going too far.'

For the first time expression moved Ryan's features. 'You want to warn *me*?' He laughed, coarsely. 'Against what? Swenson and his half-assed crew?'

Burnett let him enjoy the laugh before he shook his head again, 'Nope. Just one of them.'

Ryan scowled. 'You mean Billy.'

'Billy,' Burnett agreed. 'Look, Ryan, you've got the game won. You've taken the only part of Horn that matters a damn to you. Let Swenson keep his pride. It costs you nothing. Don't finish this the way you're planning to.'

'Why don't you tell Swenson? He's the sorehead.'

'Because it wouldn't do any good. You wouldn't let it do any good. You'll ride him until he's kill-crazy, and then you'll smash him.'

'Name what will stop me from doing just that?' Ryan challenged.

'Nothing,' Burnett answered, flatly. 'Not one damn thing in this world can stop you, Jason, but yourself. That's why I'm here.'

'Wasting both our time,' Ryan returned, impatiently. 'You've had your say. I don't give a damn for Swenson, or you, or Billy Boy Bascom. I should have hung the little bastard first that day. But he'll follow Swenson to hell, and the sooner the better.'

Pete Burnett shook his head. He dropped the cigarette to the floor and stepped on it. 'So long as Billy's following Swenson, you don't have to worry, Jason. But you'll kill Swenson, and you'll either kill or scare off his hired guns. But you won't kill Billy. He'll be left alone. Until now, he's been fighting another man's way – first Trumbull, then Swenson. He'll be on his own then, and he'll go after you his own way. I don't want that to happen – for Billy's sake, not yours. You've never seen the kind of hell that lives inside Billy Bascom; if you drive him into a corner, it will break loose, and the things he'll do to get at you will turn your stomach. He won't be in a hurry, and he won't fight fair or in the open like other men. But before he's through with you, you'll wish to hell you'd never been born.'

'You're crazy, Burnett,' Ryan said, slowly.

For a moment Burnett stood there, then he lifted his shoulders in a shrug. 'I've done my best to stop you. I guess I was a damn fool to even try.'

He turned and walked back to the door. Jerry Lanham was still leaning against the building. His eyes stared sullenly into Burnett's, then Pete passed him, went down the steps. The flesh of his back crawled as he crossed the street, but he did not hurry his long stride.

He was sweating when he reached the ranch wagon. He climbed to the spring seat, unlooped the reins and kicked the handbrake free. Then he wheeled the team in a tight turn and guided them into the street. The Triangle men watched him from hard eyes as he drove out of town.

For the third time in the past hour, Billy Bascom saw Nils Swenson turn in the saddle to stare belligerently back at them.

'Goddamn it, why can't you keep up?' he shouted. 'Always draggin' your tails behind.'

Brooding anger had eaten into him, twisting permanent lines of sullenness into his heavy features. The threat of Ryan's full force being thrown at them was a constant pressure upon him, and he was breaking beneath the strain of it. Unsure of himself and how far he could trust the men about him, Swenson made no attempt at running Horn; he sent the men, day after day, on endless line-riding, and kept a twenty-four hour watch on the ranch. His temper, never even, had crumbled into a steady, bitter rage, and it was in Billy's mind that almost anything might send the big man into a berserker fury that would give Ryan the excuse he was waiting for to attack.

Hank Lewis watched Swenson steadily. 'Ridin' blind in this country will get you killed,' he said.

'If you're afraid, damn you, why'd you hire on?' Swenson returned, angrily. 'Goddamn it, as long as you're workin' for me, you'll stir your lazy bones.'

Lewis shrugged. 'Maybe you'd better give me my time,' he said. 'Stirrin' up dust ridin' line, lettin' Triangle riders do as they damned please, ain't my idea of standin' up to Ryan.'

'Sure, damn you, quit an' run out!' Swenson bellowed. 'The whole bunch of you can go to hell for all of me!' Furiously, he whirled his horse and sent the animal plunging down the slope toward the distant Horn buildings.

Lewis watched him go, then shook his head. 'A man with some sense might stand a chance against Ryan, but we ain't workin' for one. Two stinkin' months, ridin' our tails off, four of us carryin'' lead from Triangle snipin' – an' every time there's a chance for a showdown, Swenson backs away from it.'

'Maybe he's right, even if he don't know it,' Billy replied. He shaped a cigarette, lit it and squinted at the broad horizon. The last of the dry, hot summer was ending, and the winter rains would be coming. 'If I was Ryan, I'd like nothin' better than Swenson to jump me all-out. I'd finish it, once an' for all. One mistake an' Swenson – an' every damned one of us ridin' for him – is done for.'

'So he's so damned afraid he'll do the wrong thing, he does nothin' at all.' Lewis spat scornfully to the ground.

Billy frowned and flipped the cigarette away. Across the distant horizon a smudge of dust was spreading. He watched it for a moment. 'Somebody drivin' a rig out the road from Lanyard. We better get down there.'

'That mean you're stickin' it out with Swenson?'

Billy nodded. 'I won't cut an' run. If we pull out, Ryan will kill him inside an hour.'

Lewis hesitated a moment, then shrugged. 'Hell, you're right, but I'm thinkin' the only difference it's goin' to make is Swenson's goin' to have our company on the ride to hell.'

They put their horses to the slope and rode into Horn, past the fire-blackened walls of the ranch house. Swenson had taken over the big bunkhouse, but had made no effort to rebuild any of the fire damage. The rancher's big bay stood in the middle of the yard, and Swenson was standing, legs apart, glaring down the road. A fan-top buggy wheeled along, driven by a small, thin man in dark clothes.

'Trouble for sure,' Lewis said. 'That's Hiram Daly, Judge Mowery's clerk, an' he hates Swenson's guts. Him an' the Swede have tangled before.'

The buggy came into the yard and pulled up as Billy dismounted. Jake Haley, sitting sprawled on a bench siding the bunkhouse, grinned up at him.

'The Swede's so goddamn mad you can see him oozin' it.'

Two or three of Swenson's hired guns were idling at the front of the building, watching Swenson as the big man moved belligerently toward the buggy.

'What toadyin' you doin' for Ryan out here, Daly?' Swenson demanded.

Hiram Daly, a pinch-faced man with a cold stare, replied sharply, 'Judge Mowery sent me. This is for you.' He leaned out of the buggy to hand a folded paper to Swenson. The rancher took it, then glared at the smaller man.

'What is it?'

Daly's thin face moved in a smirk. His intense dislike of the big man was obvious. He was enjoying Swenson's anger to the utmost, and showed it. 'It's a ruling of the Territorial Court, recognizing Ryan's claim against Trumbull.' The little man leaned further from the buggy to hurl his taunting words at Swenson. 'You've lost out, damn you, Swenson! You'll get off this land, or they'll put you off!'

The red drained from Swenson's face, then he ripped the paper viciously in half.

'Fat lot of good that'll do you!' Daly shrilled out. His braying laughter mingled with the screech of the wheels as he slapped the reins and urged the horse into a tight turn.

For an instant Swenson stood there, the veins on his forehead purpling, then he yelled an insane curse, and dragged his gun free of the holster. Billy sprang forward, but a single shot slammed out before he could grab Swenson's arm. The black fan-top of the buggy jerked to the impact of lead, then Daly's slight form pitched into the dirt of the road and lay still. The buggy rolled on a few feet, then slowed to a stop.

Swenson, his insane rage suddenly gone, stared at the still form in the dusty road, then down at the gun in his hand. He turned slowly to look at Billy, making an odd, despairing movement with his other hand.

Before he could speak, one of Swenson's riders behind them grunted with pain, and, even as he started to fall, there sounded the distant, spiteful crack of a rifle. Billy jerked around. A second rifle thundered from a ridge a quarter-mile away. Hank Lewis ran toward him. Swenson still stared down at the dead man, unaware of what was happening.

'My God, it's Ryan's whole outfit!' Lewis yelled. 'This is what they've been waitin' for!'

A dozen horsemen topped the distant ridge, riding in. More appeared. Billy shot a quick glance about him, taking in the bunkhouse from which other Swenson men were running, wild-eyed. His hand caught Swenson's arm in a grip that made the bigger man wince with pain and stare into his face.

'Listen to me!' Billy shouted. 'You've given Ryan the excuse he needed. Now you've got to fight. But not here! Get into town – your own place. Maybe he won't risk a showdown right in town. It's the only chance we've got. You hear me?'

Swenson's eyes were dazed, but he nodded. 'Sure, Billy sure,' he replied. Behind them, some of their own men were firing at the oncoming riders.

'Break an' run for it!' Billy yelled. 'Get back to Lanyard, an' Swenson's store! We'll make a stand there. Now scatter!'

A second man sagged back against the adobe-walled bunkhouse, leaving a bloodstain on the dirty adobe as he fell. The others broke and ran. Billy saw Swenson leap for his horse, swing up. Under the pressure of constant threat he had broken, but now it was different. His face was set and hard, and the revolver in his hand bucked again and again. One of the oncoming riders threw up his hands and pitched from the saddle. The others kept on, firing as they came. Bullets chewed into the walls of the bunkhouse. A window broke with a crash. Horses screamed in fright.

Lewis and Haley ran with Billy, and were with him when he mounted and swung his horse into the yard. He pulled his rifle from the boot, and opened a steady fire down the road. One horse reared and fell, pinning its rider. The others scattered, pulling back. Then the Swenson men rode out, singly and in pairs. Billy emptied the rifle, then wheeled the mare.

'Let's go!' he shouted.

He saw Swenson, riding like a madman, up the slope. Then Haley and Lewis with him, Billy put the mare in a different direction, and drove in his spurs. Rifles cracked behind him, and he saw slugs plough the dirt ahead of him, and the vicious hum of leaden death was all about him. They topped the rise and swung down the far side, and the sound of shots faded behind then. Once, when he paused to look back, he saw there was no pursuit and his mouth was a thin, grim line when he rode on.

Jason Ryan rode into the Horn ranch yard and pulled up. He looked once at the fire-blackened walls of the main building, then turned in the saddle to stare out across the grasslands. For a moment he held there, face flushed, his hands knotted at his side. He had taken no active part in the brief, bitter fight, but the victory was his alone.

Beside him the lanky frame of Jem Mace sat stiffly erect. 'Five men dead,' the sheriff said, bitterly. 'Three of your Triangle riders, two of Swenson's men. That's a hell of a price to pay for a piece of land.'

'But not a tenth of what I'll spend if I have to,' Jason returned, flatly. His eyes were as hard as the glint of ice in the sun. 'I'll finish this. The grab-and-hold days are ending now; this is the last chance I'll have. Ten years from now, how I got what I have will be forgotten. The Trumbulls and the Swensons and all the rest will mean nothing to me or anyone else. So why should they mean anything to me now?'

Mace stared at the other man for an instant. 'It's your show,' he said, finally. 'Swenson an' his men got away. They've scattered all over hell. You want us to go after them?'

Ryan shook his head slowly. 'No. Swenson will head for Lanyard. He'll hole up in his store. His men – those who don't just keep on riding – will gather there. Swenson's gambling I haven't the guts to finish it in town.' The coldness of his face was inhuman. 'It's a bet he'll lose.'

Silence as thick as a blanket of fog filled the streets of Lanyard, and the saloons and store fronts were dark and shuttered. The absence of normal night noises – the barking of dogs, the tinny plinking of pianos, the occasional loud burst of laughter or angry yells – left a vacuum that was filled with a growing tension. Billy was aware of the silence, of the nerve-fraying tension, as he stood to one side of the long kitchen in the adobe-walled section of Swenson's place.

Swenson sat at the head of the table, his head in his hands. Only three of his men had ridden into town, and they were uneasy, restless.

'Six of us,' Jake Haley said. He squatted, his back against one thick wall. 'It don't look good to me, kid.'

Billy frowned. 'It could be worse,' he answered. 'But don't ask me how. It's a cinch worryin' about it won't help. How about you spellin' Hank at the gate? I'll relieve you in two hours.'

Jake grimaced. 'What about Swenson an' his crew takin' a turn?'

'You goin' to sleep while one of them keeps watch?' Billy asked.

Jake shook his head, grinned wryly, and climbed to his feet. He moved toward the door. The screen door slammed behind him, the noise racketing in the quiet room. At the table, Swenson lifted his head, wearily.

'All my life it's been a hard scrabble,' he said. 'I never got anything without workin' twice as hard as it was worth. It was like that when I came to Lanyard twenty years ago. Ryan had everything. A man got in his way, he knocked him out of it. Me, I tried to play the game square. A hell of a lot it's got me.'

The screen door squeaked, and Hank Lewis came in. He blinked in the lamplight, nodded grimly, and moved to the stove. He lifted the black pot, poured coffee into a mug and carried it to the table. He eased down onto the bench. He ignored Swenson.

'Triangle's comin' into town, Billy,' he said. 'Twos an' threes, keepin' quiet, shyin' clear of here. The Ryan-Dolan store's lit up like a Christmas tree.' He blew on the coffee, sipped cautiously. 'Seen Mace an' Oringer ride in. Bob give us a look; Mace rode like a man with his head in a sack.'

Swenson stood up slowly, heavily. 'Billy, maybe you an' the others better make a run for it. Ryan will settle for me.'

'Pour yourself another cup of coffee,' Billy said. He didn't look at the big man. 'Ryan had this town boxed ten minutes after we rode in.'

Swenson blinked, then sat down again. 'What'll we do, kid?'

Billy sipped at his coffee, built a cigarette, and squinted as he lit it. 'We'll wait,' he said, flatly. 'You got any guns in the store? Get 'em.'

Swenson got up and moved to the inside door, hesitated there. 'Frank, you come along with me. I'll need some help.' One of Swenson's sullen-faced men stood up. They went through the door into the store.

Hank Lewis drained his cup, got up to refill it. He came back and sat down. 'This is a hell of a mess. I always figgered, I get in a jam, I can always cut an' run. It don't look likely now. Ryan ain't goin' to throw us in the clink. He's got somethin' a hell of a lot more permanent in mind.'

'We'll take any break we see,' Billy said. 'I thought ridin' into town would give us breathin' time. I was wrong.'

Hank Lewis frowned heavily. 'Trouble is, Ryan's too big for little men to buck.'

Billy shook his head. 'Just too big for honest little men,' he said. 'I get out here in one piece, I got other ideas.'

'Me an' Jake figgered it like that. We come out of this with you, we'll go along.'

Billy's white teeth flashed in his crooked half-smile. 'Ryan hung my last two pards,' he said, quietly, watching Lewis' face. 'I never thought I could hate any man the way I hate Jason Ryan. He's standin' so tall his shadow makes it night. I hate his guts. I hate his smell. I'd crawl across the coals of hell on my naked belly to get a chance at him. I'd shoot a horse he rode. I'd poison a dog that answered his call. There just ain't nothin' else in this stinkin' world I want more than to hit back at Ryan and make him feel it. I want him to know what it's like to get hurt bad, to be scared, to run with his tail between his legs. I want it so bad I can taste it.' Billy stopped, and his hand about the crockery mug was white with pressure. 'You can't name the thing I won't do to bring Ryan down.'

For an instant their eyes locked, and then, with complete finality, Lewis said, 'That makes two of us.'

The third man in the room came over to the table. His name was Grant Myers, he hailed from Texas, he wore a gun like he wore his hat, and his face was as blank of expression as the shell of an egg.

'This stinks,' he said. 'Why should I stick around?'

Hank Lewis grinned scornfully. 'Because you damn well can't get out.'

Myer's thin-lipped mouth moved into a silent snarl, and he backed away from the table. Feet clumped beyond the inner door, and Swenson and the other man came in. They were carrying two rifles each, and their pockets bulged with shells.

'I locked the store. The street's empty outside,' Swenson reported.

The two hired guns moved across the room and sat in back-tilted chairs against the far wall. They began to talk together in low tones. Swenson sat down, silently began to raise and lower his clenched fists, his face a brooding mask. The coffee pot rumbled on the stove. The two men across the room stopped whispering, their string of talk run out, their sullen thoughts reflected in the shine of their eyes as they watched Swenson.

The thin sound of distant hoofs whispered in. Swenson lifted his head. The other men listened. The sound of a running horse grew louder.

Like the slam of a fist against a door at midnight, gunshots shattered the quiet of the night. A horse screamed with fright and pain. Running feet pounded frantically. Rifles rolled thunder over the sleeping town of Lanyard. The screen door banged open, and Jake Haley burst in, wild-eyed.

'Smash that damn light!' he yelled. 'One of Swenson's men tried to ride in – God, they blew him apart. Ryan's got a hundred men out there, lined up in the street like a regular army.'

Billy drew his revolver, and blew out the lamp. Blackness blinked about them, streaked with the soft, red glow of the low fire in the grate of the stove. In the wake of the shattering roar of the rifles, uneasy silence fell, murky with the threat of violence. Then it was gone, and bullets crashed into the thick, adobe walls. Glass broke with a crash. Men cursed. One of Swenson's men was at the window, firing crazily into the night.

Billy moved unhurriedly to the window, held his body to one side, and studied the darkness outside for several seconds. Moonlight lay across the space between the building and the adobe wall that faced the street. He saw men hurrying across the street, heard shouted cries, saw the firefly-blink of guns. The noise of the fusillade was like the heavy drumming of falling water. The wall in front of him quivered to the impact of lead. A bullet found a chink in sun-dried adobe and screeched into the room to smash against the stove with a clang like the stroke of a hammer against an anvil. Billy rested his gun hand on the high sill of the window. He saw the dark, hurrying shadow of a man, and felt the Colt buck against his fingers. The shadow jerked erect, fell heavily.

Behind him a man screeched with pain, then fell cursing crazily. Billy found another target, fired and saw the running man stumble and fall, then roll frantically for cover. Most of the attackers had crossed the street and gained the shelter of the wall, and the red flames of guns topped its length.

Grant Myer's voice pitched shrilly, shouted, 'To hell with this crap!' Billy swivelled his head, saw the man burst through the screen door, his gun blazing.

'Cover him!' Billy yelled, and fired as rapidly as he could thumb the hammer of his gun. He saw Myers break for the far end of the wall toward the stables. Swenson's hired gun was moving fast, his long legs driving like pistons. Then gunshots rattled like a stick against a picket fence in the hands of a running boy, and Myers' legs went rubbery. He kept going a pace or two, then hurtled down, torn to pieces.

The firing ceased on both sides, as if the death of Grant Myers were a signal. Billy thumbed cartridges into the hammers of his revolver. In the darkness of the room, someone was praying. It struck Billy odd to realize it was Nils Swenson.

The silence held for long seconds, then Jake Haley yelled out, 'The dirty bastards have fired the warehouse – smell the smoke?'

Through the narrow rectangle of the window, Billy saw a yellow-red glare flicker on the face of the buildings across the street. Windowpanes reflected flames that pyramided into the sky. Thick, billowing smoke, caught by a downdraft of wind, roiled into the street, and men cursed and began to cough. Rifles racketed again, and bullets dug into the thick, adobe walls. Billy held his fire, eyes squinted. The smoke eddied up, and the street cleared, the yellow blaze of the fire lighting it as if by sunlight. In the room, light flickered and danced up the walls, and Billy heard movement behind him, turned and saw Nils Swenson. The big man's face was set and blank. His eyes were glazed.

'A man never has a chance for the things he wants,' he said, slowly. 'Not a stinkin' chance. You crawl small all you life an' never stop. When you try to stand up, there's always somebody waitin' to knock you down.' His white face broke and twisted. 'The whole goddamn world is one big stink. I need fresh air.'

Swenson dropped his rifle to the floor and walked to the door.

Jake Haley yelled, 'Stop the crazy bastard!'

Billy held still, then slowly shook his head. 'What good would it do?' he asked fiercely.

Swenson didn't hear them. His big shoulders filled the doorway, and he stepped outside, walking slowly. Billy turned to the window. He saw Swenson walking toward the wall. Smoke billowed down about him and he walked through it. For an instant that seemed to last forever, the big man walked into smoky silence. Then a voice raised in a shout. It was Jason Ryan, and Billy would remember the glass-hard tones as long as he lived.

'Leave him alone!' Ryan commanded. 'He's mine!'

Swenson reached the midway point between the building and the wall and turned to look toward his burning store. The harsh light of the flames outlined him like the beam of a searchlight. He raised both fists high over his head in a stance of terrible and futile anger.

'Turn around, Swenson!' Ryan called out. 'I want to see your face!'

The big man remained still an instant longer, then wheeled slowly. Even as his shoulders turned to face the wall, a single rifle shot cracked. The bullet caught Swenson in the belly, doubled him forward like the slam of a giant's fist. Both hands clutched his stomach and he staggered forward. The rifle roared again, and again, and the bullets jerked the big man's body. His steps faltered, slowed; even his great strength could not keep him on his feet. He was humbled, and sank down like a man kneeling to pray.

The rifle spoke a final, bitter time, driving Swenson's head back, and he tumbled into the dirt of the street, knees drawn up, like a sleeping child.

For an instant Billy held there, his face drawn tight, then he said, softly, 'Time to go. All of us at once. The stable is covered for sure, but there'll be horses on the street. Don't waste your shots. The more of them you drop, the better your chance. Get ready!'

The flames were standing straight up into the sky. Ugly, black smoke boiled out and was whipped into the air by the wind. Billy wheeled like a cat.

'Now!' he called, and ran for the door.

Haley and Lewis and the last of Swenson's men moved fast. Billy stood to one side of the door. 'All right, Hank, run for it! Jake, you next – then you! Run, damn you!'

The thick, grey-black smoke clogged their nostrils, made them choke for breath. They vanished into it at a run. Guns thundered crazily. Billy hesitated there in the doorway for a moment longer. The smoke was thinning. His twisted, bitter smile appeared. He stepped through the door, saw men leaning over the wall, firing at the runners ahead of him. Like a man on a target range, Billy took time to aim and fire, quick, careful shots. Dust exploded atop the adobe wall. He glimpsed one man reeling back, his face a bloody pulp. A second screamed in terrible agony and dropped from sight.

The firing along the wall stopped as men ducked down frantically. Billy's smile widened, and his lithe legs carried him in a run. He heard a man yell curses; hoofs pounded in the street; then Billy was past the burning warehouse and plunging into the sheltering darkness beyond. Lights flickered in windows. He saw white, frightened faces staring down at the street-fighting. Horses milled and stamped in panic. Then a man appeared in front of him, raising a revolver.

Billy went down in a crouch, and the explosion of the cartridge burned his back. Then he was inside, coming up, the barrel of his empty revolver driven like the point of a knife into the man's throat. He felt the sickening crunch as the gun barrel tore in, driven by the full force of his body. The man uttered one croaking cry, then went over backward. Billy straddled him, struck with the heavy revolver viciously again and again. For an instant he held there, panting. In the shadowy red glare of the fire, he saw Jerry Lanham's bloody, distorted face. On Lanham's open vest a silver star shone dully. Billy bent, ripped it free, clenched it in his doubled fist, then turned and jumped for a horse.

The animal shied, but Billy's catlike quickness enabled him to mount. He jerked the reins free, wheeled the horse. Behind him, rifles were thundering again, sweeping the street. Ryan's men were kill-crazy, firing blindly. A horse at the rail reared and lunged over backward, striking out with pain-crazed hoofs. Others broke free, and Billy's mount ran with them. For an instant the lighted windows of Lanyard blurred past him, and then they were gone. He was in the darkness beyond the town, riding hard.

CHAPTER 9

Two hours before dawn, Billy doubled back toward Lanyard. When the lights of the town lay below him, a sparse sprinkling of soft, yellow stars against the black sea of the grasslands, he reined in. The harsh stench of the fire yet tainted the still warmth of the night, and occasional showers of sparks marked where Swenson's store had stood.

Ryan would be riding high now, Billy thought, bitterly. Lanyard County would be his own private empire, and he would patrol it with men ordered to kill on sight any of the surviving Swenson riders. Hank Lewis and Jake Haley had headed for a line camp high in the hills where they would remain for a week – or until Billy met them there. Before morning he would be well on his way to meet them, but in the meantime he had one last thing to do. Frowning, he urged on the horse.

He rode close beside the broken wire fence that bordered the cemetery, and, coming to a place between two sagging posts where the wire had fallen, rode through. He dismounted and led the horse toward Harry Trumbull's grave. He found the low mound, already beginning to sink, and halted. He dropped the reins to the ground and pushed his hat back from his face. He rolled a cigarette, shielded the flare of the match, then leaped suddenly to one side in a silent, deadly movement that also saw his revolver drawn and levelled.

'Hello, kid,' Pete Burnett's quiet voice said from the darkness beyond the grave. 'I've been waiting for you.'

Billy holstered the revolver slowly. 'That's a good way to get yourself killed, Pete,' he replied. 'The quicker I shoot, the longer I'll stay alive.'

'I know that, Billy. It's why I came. I had a hunch you'd come here before you started what you're goin' to do.'

'Nothing you've got to say is goin' to stop me, Pete.' Billy's voice was cold.

Boots crunched gravel, and Burnett's tall form loomed against the lights of the town. 'You made your try, kid, but it didn't work. You were doin' it Swenson's way. I'd hate to see you attempt it your own way. Trumbull gave you a start on something new, something I'd like to see grow.'

'Ryan stomped it into the ground.'

'Not if you'll face it out. Go away, start over again. Use a different name. It can be done.'

'I doubt it.' Billy spoke slowly, matter of factly. 'This is an old story to me, Pete. I've been through it before. I've seen you and other men make it work for them. Sometimes I've even hated your guts because it seemed so easy for you. You walk tall, and you ride tall, and you make men see it. They know you'll hit back hard if they force you to a fight, and they respect you for it. The same men sneer openly every time they see my face. It's the difference between you an' me. It doesn't matter how many men I kill; there's always another one who has to try his luck.'

'You were making it work with Trumbull.'

'Yeah, I was.' Billy's voice deepened. 'Because that's the kind of man he was – so much more than I could ever be, just walkin' beside him made me feel bigger than I ever felt before. He made no show about bein' what he was. He never threw a brag, never cursed a man out, an' never hurt a thing in his life.' Billy stopped. 'Then there's me. I've killed fourteen men – fifteen, if I hit Jerry Lanham as hard as I intended to.'

'You did. He's dead,' Burnett said.

'Uhuh. Fifteen. You see how easy it is to say? It's just a number, a pretty small one. By itself it don't mean nothin'. But it isn't just a number, Pete. Fifteen times I've killed a man. It should make me sick to even think about it, but it doesn't. If you had the record, it would tie your guts in knots. It even bothers me. I've cut an' run to keep from killin' more. Maybe that ain't much credit to me, but it's all I got. I never knowin'ly killed a man with a family. I never killed a man just for the sake of killin', but I'm goin' to, just once, when I kill Jason Ryan. But I ain't in no hurry. I'm goin' to worry him, cut him down to size, an' just when he thinks he's got everythin' he wants, I'm goin' to cut him down an' hear him scream.' The hard, flat voice stopped.

'It sounds real fine an' proud, Billy,' Burnett said. 'But you're kiddin' yourself. You'll start out with high ideas, an' maybe live up to them for a while. But you'll need money an' you won't have time to work for it. You'll steal. You'll keep tellin' yourself you're fightin' a war all by yourself, fightin' for what's right, makin' a bastard like Ryan know he can't grab just as he pleases. But you can't fool yourself forever. You'll see yourself changin' into a lobo wolf, killin' anything that gets in your way. You'll be worse than Ryan could ever be. And you'll have to be stopped.'

'Not until I get Ryan,' Billy cut in, coldly. 'I wouldn't want you to be the one to try, Pete.'

'Time will take care of men like Ryan, kid – it doesn't need your help. I'm goin' to do what I have to do, and I wouldn't want you on the other side. That's why I came here tonight. I've got a little

97

spread beyond the Torollones. I need a good hand. Ride back with me.'

For a moment silence held between them. 'It wouldn't work out, Pete,' Billy said, finally. 'Together we would make a force against Ryan he'd have to smash. I'm doin' it my way.'

He knelt beside the wooden marker over Trumbull's grave. He dug into his pocket, found what he sought. It was the badge he had ripped from the dead Lanham's vest. He opened the pin, set it atop the crossbar of the wooden cross, then drove the point into the soft wood with a shove of his hand. The star glistened dully in the darkness.

'That's the first one,' Billy said, softly. He stood erect, turned abruptly away.

'Wait, Billy!' Burnett called out. But the silent figure of the kid backed into the night, and an instant later the hoofs of his horse pounded away.

Bob Oringer was aware of the subdued air that had came to the town of Lanyard, just as he was aware of the new deference, amounting almost to fright, that was shown him as he paced the main street. In his new suit and boots, with the shining deputy's star on his chest, he cut a fine figure and knew it. His right leg still bothered him at times, and he affected a limp that amounted to a swagger. There was no disgrace in the fact that he carried a piece of lead from Billy Bascom's gun in his leg; the kid's reputation made his own that much brighter. He had faced the kid and lived. Even more, he had forced the young outlaw to run. The thought pleased Oringer, and he smiled as he walked.

To add to his self-satisfaction, Jason Ryan had spent an hour in private with him that morning, making it clear he was counting on Oringer's help. The two-bit ranchers of the valley would have a surprise in store for them if they thought Ryan would be satisfied with smashing Trumbull and Swenson. And Jem Mace and his ill-concealed dislike for what was being done wouldn't last long. The sheriff's gold badge, Oringer thought, would look just right on his chest....

He came abreast the clapboard-sided building that housed the county court as well as the sheriff's office and jail. This latter comprised the front half of the second storey, a small office and a single, long room partitioned by iron bars for the jail proper. To one side of the open double doors that led into the courthouse was nailed the bulletin board, shielded meagerly from sun and rain by a shingled overhang. Oringer stopped and eyed the fly-specked posters. Then, grinning, he pried four thumbtacks free, took a paper from his pocket and pinned it to the board.

WANTED FOR MURDER

William H. Bascom,
Alias 'Billy Boy,'
Alias 'The Kid'

$500 REWARD $500

He admired the poster for a moment, pulling a cigar from a vest pocket and lighting it.

'Blood money,' a soft voice said behind him, and Oringer wheeled about.

He grinned into Conchita Noriega's dark-skinned, oval face. 'It'll still buy what you want to spend it for,' he replied. 'That's the first offer. If it doesn't get results, it'll grow. Each time you put a zero behind it, it's that much harder to laugh it off. You ever think about what a few thousand iron men would do for you, sweetheart?'

A shadow of a frown narrowed the space between her brows, then her slender shoulders lifted in a shrug. 'You talk like a fool.'

'You think so?' His smile grew wider. 'Times change, baby. A year ago you couldn't see me for dust. It was all 'Billito' then, but now ...' His expression changed, went hard, and he grabbed her wrist. 'Just don't wait too long to make up your mind, *amada mia.*'

She shook her arm free, stared into his eyes for a moment longer, then turned and walked away, her red-varnished high heels clicking against the sidewalk. Oringer watched the lithe swing of her hips, the natural grace of her body, with animal hunger in his eyes.

Paul Dorman came out of the open double doors of the court-house, chewing on a strand of straw. His ugly face was unshaven, his rough clothes dirty. The deputy's star pinned to his red-wool shirt was filmed with greasy dirt. He grinned crookedly after the girl. 'You're goin' to wind up payin' a damn high price for that,' he observed, dryly.

'Am I?' Oringer turned slowly. 'Shows who's the damn fool. Five hundred bucks ain't enough, but wait until it jumps to twenty times as much. And if I know the kid, it won't take him long to get the ante raised. For that kind of money she'd sell her soul. Puttin' Billy Bascom's head in a noose won't stand in her way. Wait an' see!'

Three men pushed a small, bunched herd through the soft, warm, night rain that beat steadily against their ponchos. The going rate, Billy mused thoughtfully, was close to thirty dollars a head for fat steers, but he would be lucky to get twenty from Bentley. Still, the army cattle buyer wasn't fussy about brands, and the night's work would net the three men a thousand silver cartwheels to jingle in their Levis. With some of it, they could stock the line shack with provisions and use it as a base of operations to start cutting at Ryan's empire. It was a damned small beginning, Billy reflected soberly. To a man who ran better than forty thousand head of cattle on his own land, it was less than the pestering of a fly.

Billy frowned. Twice in the past three weeks he had seen Triangle line riders and worked down into rifle range, only to have them turn tail at the first shot. The first time it had puzzled him; the second time he had felt a growing concern. Then there was the simple fact that although Ryan had posted a reward for him, dead or alive, no active effort had been made to take him or run him off. It almost seemed like Ryan was ignoring him, or using him in some obscure way to further his own aims. This cutting out of the herd tonight – it had been too simple, as if Ryan didn't give a damn about what Billy Bascom did. Billy had checked every possibility of a trap, and found none, Apart from the iron ring of watchers he kept posted around the main buildings of Triangle, Ryan paid Billy no attention at all.

A year ago, Billy would have called Ryan a damned fool and laughed about it; but he had learned bitter lessons about the viciousness of human nature and felt Jason Ryan would most likely demonstrate a few more.

Ahead of them showed a flicker of yellow lamplight, and Billy urged his horse to one side. The dark shape of Jake Haley loomed up, his rubber poncho glistening in the rain. 'There's Maxton's,' Billy said. 'Bed 'em down here. I'll ride in. Bentley should be there. We'll be out of here in a couple of hours, then we'll ride for El Paso.'

Without waiting for a reply, he turned his horse, and rode around the slow-moving, head-down herd. A double row of lights grew clearer, outlining a large building. Although he had called Ben Maxton a friend for most of his life, coming here always depressed Billy.

Colonel Ben Maxton was the last of the filibusters who had ridden into the Territory when it was still a Spanish province. For 200 years the Gregorio hacienda had been a way-stop on El Comino Real, and later a stage station on the Santa Fe Trail. The hospitality of the Maxton House had once been the talk of the frontier. At the great tables more than 200 guests at a time had been fed. Kit Carson had called Ben Maxton his best friend, and the Colonel did not number an enemy in the West. Americans, *Tejanos*, Mexicans, Indians – all men were welcome at the Maxton House, and even now, at the end of the Colonel's days, when he was bedfast and sick, he never turned away a hungry man. And, despite the fact that the holdings he had once counted by the hundred-thousand acres had shrunk to meagre hundreds and his gigantic herds had dwindled from theft and butchery to a sparse few, Ben Maxton still held no man his enemy.

Billy circled the big house; the stables were badly lit by a single lantern, and there was no sign of a hostler. Billy reined in and considered the house carefully. The Maxton House had fallen upon

101

sorry days, and there were few signs of its former glory. The veranda that squatted across the front sagged, and one upright pillar was missing, giving the place a gap-toothed look. But the windows were alight as cheerfully as when Don Ben had been host to the entire Southwest. After a moment, Billy turned the horse back to the stable. He rode in, dismounted, found a canvas feed bag, scraped up oats from the bottom of a bin and turned the animal, still saddled, into a stall. The smell of death and decay was strong, and he stepped hastily out into the rain.

He walked to the back of the big house, alert but seeing nothing to arouse his suspicions. There had been a half-dozen horses in the stable, but none of them wet or lathered from recent use. He stepped onto the creaking boards of the back porch, stood to one side to peer through a window into the big kitchen. The huge, clay stoves that had once cooked whole oxen to feed hungry travellers stood dark and empty; a single, low hearth held coals, and he saw a tall, thin Indian woman bending to stir them.

Billy opened a torn screen door, and the woman turned to regard him solemnly. 'Hello, Juanita,' Billy said.

The Indian woman's face remained dark stone. 'Señor Bentley is with Don Ben,' she said in Spanish.

He nodded and passed through the kitchen to the dark hall beyond. A few dingy tapestries remained on dirty stucco walls that were peeling scabrously. The hall ended at a wide foyer where several candles flickered fitfully, the light glittering on the begrimed, broken crystals of a huge chandelier. The smell of death filled the house, a raw, ugly scent that gathered thickly about him.

He went through the open double doors into the study beyond. Here the onslaught of time and decay had been fought savagely. Mexican rugs, thick and violent with colour, spilled across the hand-set tile floor; the twenty-foot fireplace held a blazing log; glass-shaded lamps burned on dark, fine-wood tables. Over the fireplace hung a life size portrait of Doña Ysabella, once mistress of an empire, her beauty untouched by time. Facing the fire, in a huge wing chair, his wasted legs covered by a dark wool rug, sat the white-haired Ben Maxton. His lean, hawk-like features were sagging, the white skin crisscrossed with a million fine lines, but his eyes were bright and undimmed.

A second man, dark and squat, sat in a straight chair, frowning into the fire. He looked up, then stood quickly. 'You're late,' he said, half-angrily.

'That's better than never,' Billy replied. He came forward, shucking off his poncho. He laid it on a wooden chair. 'Howdy, Ben.'

Maxton smiled. 'Billy, my son, it's good to see you. It's been a long time.'

'Not so long until next time,' Billy answered, and gripped the pale hand.

Maxton's sharp eyes held to the kid's face. 'Are you returning to your old ways, Billy? I've heard some ugly things. Jason Ryan …'

Billy shook his head and smiled. 'Nothin's ever as bad as it's painted.'

Bentley whispered, urgently, 'You got them cows?'

Billy nodded. 'Fifty head. Haley an' Lewis are with 'em just north of here. Send your men after them. Let Haley an' Lewis ride in for chow. We're beat.'

Bentley grinned crookedly. 'Done.' He left the room. Billy took the chair he had vacated.

The Colonel dozed in the warmth of the fire. Billy relaxed, letting the peace of the room fill him. Time held no meaning here. A man could think, take a while to get his bearings, see where he was going.

Juanita came silently into the room, and Billy stood up, followed her back to the kitchen. She had set a place at the end of a table. He sat down. Two empty plates waited for Haley and Lewis. Billy grinned his thanks and dug into he food she dished up for him. He drank his coffee. When she came to refill his cup, he looked into her eyes. 'How is he, Juanita?'

The dark face softened for one tiny instant, and her eyes filled with pain and sorrow that vanished even before he could be sure it was there. She shook her head. '¿Quién sabe? There is so little left … if it will but last until he is gone …'

'It has to,' Billy said. Then the screen door banged, and the woman moved back into the shadows of the room.

Clegg Bentley came up, dripping in a huge army-issue poncho. He pulled it off and sat down. 'OK, we're back in business, kid. Twenty dollars a head – an' I'll take all you can get. Skin a cow, an' who gives a damn what brand was on the hide? Army bellies take a lot of beef to fill. You makin' regular deliveries?'

Billy frowned. He rolled a cigarette, lit it. In the glow of the match his face was hard.

'Hell, you can steal a hundred head a month the rest of your life, an' Ryan'll never miss 'em,' Bentley urged.

That's just the trouble, Billy thought, angrily, he'll never miss them. He nodded. 'I'll let you know.'

The cattle-buyer dug into this coat, pulled out a leather bag that clinked melodiously. 'A thousand in gold, kid. Play it smart, an' you'll get rich.' He winked ponderously, then went out.

Juanita came back, face expressionless. Billy drew the leather bag toward him, loosened the drawstrings, dumped the gold coins into his hand. He counted out five, dumped the rest back, closed the bag and stuck it into his shirt. He laid the five golden coins on the table. 'Spread it thin, Juanita. Keep things goin' for Ben as long as you can.' He stood up. 'Jake an' Hank will be in after a while. Let them eat. My old room still fixed up?'

The black eyes glistened with unshed tears of gratitude. 'It will always wait for you, *niño.*'

Billy smiled his thanks, then walked toward the door at the far end of the room. A candle burned in one corner of the thick-walled room beyond it. A feather-ticking bed awaited him, and he was tired. He stood still a moment and thought. A two-bit rustler should keep on the move, spread his money thin, and take no chances. A man could last a long time that way, and maybe – just maybe – he could eventually annoy a giant like Jason Ryan.

Billy's fists clenched, and his eyes closed. The tiredness slid from his shoulders, and he turned around quickly, returned to the kitchen. Juanita watched him. 'Tell Haley an' Lewis I'll meet them in El Paso. Give them this.' He dumped the leather coin bag on the table. He left the kitchen, walked down the long hall. Ben Maxton still dozed in the big chair. Billy took his poncho and hat, donned them as he returned to the back of the house. He passed through it in silence, back to the rain and night. He sloshed through the rutted mud of the yard to the stables, got his horse. The stench of death and decay seemed stronger, and he welcomed it, carried it with him as he rode away.

The ticking of the banjo clock on the wall of the sheriff's office made a steady counterpoint to the muffled snores of the drunken Mexican sleeping off a full head of tequila in one of the cells. Deputy Paul Dorman swung the chair in rhythm with the tick of the clock. He was a lank, brown-faced man not given to imaginative thinking, and with few ambitions beyond some silver to jingle in his pants and an occasional drunken spree with a Mexican girl on the line. He was oiling his new revolver bought with some of the bounty money Ryan had paid after the set-to with Swenson's outfit, and thinking half-regretfully about Jerry Lanham. Too bad his luck had run out; one thing about Jerry, he'd known how to spread his money around. Dorman thought, too, about the savage, brutal way that damn Billy Bascom had killed him, and frowned slowly.

Fear was not a part of Dorman's make-up. His emotional nature had been blighted; he could think straight and reasonably fast, but there was no link with his feelings. He knew a form of hate – for cold and rain and long night rides and drafty bunkhouses and loneliness – and for Billy Bascom, a steady hate deep inside him. But regret and sorrow had no counterpart in Paul Dorman. Sometimes the depth of emotion he saw in others puzzled him, but not much, and not for long.

The clock banged once, and he glanced up. Twelve-thirty, and Mace was late as usual. Goddamn, and with tomorrow being Sunday, Dorman had told Rosita he would show up early. His frown deepened. He wiped the last of the oil from the barrel of the gun, then swung the swivel chair around as feet thumped on the stairs and Jem Mace's slicker-clad figure emerged from the dark stair-well. Mace pushed through the low railing gate, removed his rain clothes and hung then on the clothes tree.

'I saw Oringer. He tells me Billy Bascom's taken up his old habits. Ryan's lost a bunch of cows.' Mace's hatchet-sharp face was drawn, his eyes worried.

'So what?' Dorman raised stooped shoulders in a shrug. 'The kid'll raise hell for a while, then either drift away or get hung.' He pulled on a canvas jumper, buttoned it. 'I jugged that bastard Felipe again. He tried to cut one of the girls down at Draper's. He only had six bits on him. Mowery'll have to let him work off his fine.'

Mace nodded and sat down at the desk. 'All right. Go on home.'

Dorman pushed through the railing gate, stared down the long, dark flight of stairs that led to the courthouse hall below. His back suddenly felt cold, as if rain had dripped inside his jacket. He turned to look at Mace. The sheriff was watching him, his thin face expressionless. Suddenly half-angry, Dorman went down the stairs. He reached the lower hall; a single lamp sputtered beside the closed front doors. The hall was empty, littered with dirt and crumpled papers. His footsteps echoed hollowly behind him, and the sound seemed too loud. He jerked the door open and stepped through.

Rain pushed against him. The street was puddled, and reflected light glistened like fallen stars in the mud. Scattered lighted windows were rectangular yellow patches, filtering murky glow into the rain. The boardwalk was pocked with falling rain, broken by the shadowed overhanging fronts of buildings. Dorman hesitated; Draper's place was at the south end of town, beyond the Deadline. It was a five-minute walk – and almost that far the other way to the stable where he kept his horse. He stood there, letting the rain soak into him, staring down the dark, silent street.

He cursed under his breath, then went down the steps with a belligerent swagger. His boots thumped heavily against the boardwalk. He passed the swinging doors of a saloon, caught the raw stench of stale beer and whiskey and human sweat; a piano banged noisily, and coarse laughter sounded. He reached the corner; Draper's place was two blocks away. There were no saloons between; no lights shone. The black faces of the buildings were blurred, oddly vague in detail. The rain blotted out all sound. The cold wetness slid down his spine again, and cursing didn't help. He held there, suddenly aware that he was breathing hard, nerves on edge. Goddamn it, what was the matter with him? In the darkness at the end of the street he saw the warm shine of lights. Draper's. Rosita would be there. Spangled dress, dark, red-lipped face sullenly pouting. He licked his lips. Goddamn, he needed a drink, he needed it bad. He had been doing too much thinking about that crazy Billy Bascom and what he did to Jerry Lanham....

Dorman crossed the muddy street, his back stiff, his eyes wary. He walked through every shadow on his toes, his hand inside his buttoned jumper gripping his Colt. He came to an alleyway, started across, then sensed movement and whirled, his back against a wall, his heart thumping hard. A wet, shaggy dog slipped past him, back humped, tail curled between its legs, and vanished into the night.

Dorman was shaking. He closed his eyes, breathing deeply. If this was fear, this blind, terrifying sensation, then God pity the man who walked with it always! Dorman straightened. The lights were clear now, and he could even hear the soft music of a guitar, a woman's laughter. Rosita was waiting for him, soft, warm, sensuous. A man was a goddamn fool to let fear betray him. Viciously, Dorman controlled it. He forced himself to stride straight down the boardwalk, walking without care. His back crawled at every dark doorway he passed, but he refused to look behind him. He reached the end of the block. It was easier, now. The low, adobe wall of Draper's place was just in front of him. He could hear the laughter and the noise clearly. He would be a part of it, and the taste of fear would be forgotten – and it would damn well never return! He would fight it with every bit of strength he had.

Boldly, not forcing himself, he swaggered across the street. He stepped through the open gateway in the wall, and then stopped. Yellow light spilling from an open doorway fell almost to his feet. A man stepped from the shadow of the wall, bulking monstrously in a black poncho. He stood close beside Dorman.

'It's your turn, Paul,' Billy Bascom whispered.

Paul Dorman's frozen figure jerked frantically to one side. He tried to scream, to rip his revolver free. But the long, wet-shining steel blade of Billy Bascom's knife moved faster....

Rain dripped from the lone cottonwood atop Cemetery Hill. It whispered against the ground, quickly filled each footmark of the poncho-clad man as he moved among the graves. He stopped at one wooden cross, and slowly bent down.

'That's the second one, Mr Trumbull,' Billy Bascom said, softly.

His shining, wet figure moved away. Rain fell upon the wooden cross, upon the two metal stars stuck into the wood, one dark with rust, the second still gleaming dully.

CHAPTER 10

A Mexican servant set a bowl of chilled orange and grapefruit segments in front of Governor Winston Carlisle, but the fat man's eyes did not leave the opened front page of the morning newspaper.

> *LANYARD COUNTY WAR*
> *Lawless Rampage Continues*
> *Governor Fails to Act*
> *BILLY BOY BASCOM ESCAPES*

Carlisle's thick lips tightened against his teeth. These same, damned scare-heads would be in every newspaper in the country! The arrogant tactics of Jason Ryan were enough to inspire them, but even worse, some fool had depicted that murderous boy, Billy Bascom, as a romantic desperado waging a lone-hand way against the 'Tyrant of Lanyard County'. Great gods, you'd think grown men writing and editing newspapers would laugh at the Robin Hood tales stupid Mexican peons were building about the boy!

He read on.

In the absence of any sign of positive action on the part of Governor Carlisle, a group of responsible New Mexico citizens have made an appeal to President Rutherford B. Hayes that steps be taken to end the Lanyard County War, even if Martial Law must be declared, and Governor Carlisle's appointment be ended. The name of General Lew Walton has figured prominently in the appeal.

Carlisle sucked in his breath sharply. That damned, crazy fool, Ryan, pushing too hard, driving all out for what he wanted – couldn't he see he was destroying the man he was counting on to cover up for him? Carlisle swept the paper from the table. 'Have my carriage made ready. I'm going to Lanyard today!'

Jason Ryan stood before the huge, oak-framed map of Lanyard County that almost filled the panelled wall above his wide desk, reading the story told by the little red triangle-topped pins. He picked another from the bottom of the rack, traced a line on the map and thrust it home in the centre of what had been Horn ranch.

Jem Mace's lanky shape was sprawled in a white, rawhide chair to one side. 'The kid stuck him like you'd cut a hog,' he said, harshly. 'For Christ's sake, be reasonable, Jason. With twenty men, I could get him in a week.'

Without turning around, Ryan said flatly, 'I know you could – but you won't. Leave Billy Bascom alone.'

Bob Oringer leaned against the far wall of the room, his big frame at ease. 'The kid got you spooked, Jem?'

'You're damned right he has!' the sheriff flashed. He stood up angrily. 'Bascom's kill-crazy. You realize the chance he took knifin' Dorman right in the doorway of Draper's place? Like he didn't give a damn what happened to him as long as he got his knife into Dorman first.'

Ryan swung about, his eyes fixing to Mace's face. 'I can't smash and grab without an excuse, Mace. Billy Bascom is giving me one. So long as I need him, you'll leave him alone. You understand that?'

'I'll be damned if I do!' Mace returned, savagely. 'Jason, what the hell are you trying to do?'

'Own Lanyard County, every square foot of it, every cow that walks on it, every man that rides across it.' Ryan stopped for an instant. 'Last week Bascom and his crew dynamited Three Waters. Deems Bennett owns forty sections north of there. I want that range. You will see Judge Mowery tomorrow, Mace, and get a warrant issued for Bennett's arrest, charging him with the dynamiting and with stealing Triangle cattle. Mason has drifted some cows onto Bennett's land for proof. Dolan's got some of his paper, and I'll get a writ from Mowery. You make it plain to Bennett what he's facing, and then either run him off or kill him.'

Jim Mace shook his head. 'Look, Jason....' He stopped abruptly.

'If you haven't the guts for it, send Oringer. He enjoys his work.' Ryan turned, picked up another bannered pin and thrust it savagely into the map. 'Bennett's place,' he said harshly. 'There are more. Already they've started holding meetings, sweating blood about what I'm going to do. Some hothead will set them off, or Billy Bascom will steal more cows or kill another man – and I'll smash them, every damned, stinking one of them! I've almost won. I won't stop now.'

Ryan stared at the map and did not reply. Mace stared at his back for a moment, and then shook his head. Oringer pushed himself away from the wall. 'We got work to do,' he said. 'You comin', Sheriff?'

For a moment Jem Mace hesitated, then he cursed under his breath and stood up. Ryan didn't turn around as they left.

Halfway down the grade from the pass, Pete Burnett reined in the team and studied the thick plume of smoke that arose from the flatlands below. A grass fire in this dry land was something to be feared, but this was not grass fire. Burnett frowned. The only ranch in this area belonged to Deems Bennett. The road to Lanyard struck due east here, and he could make out the brown line of it against the greening grasslands. Even as he watched, a bunched group of horsemen turned into the road and went towards Lanyard. Burnett kicked free the brake rod, and turned the team downhill. An hour later he reached the uprights that marked the turn-off to Bennett's and swung the team in.

The ranch road rounded a shoulder of the foothills, and Burnett saw the cause of the smoke. The ranch house had fallen in upon itself, a few smoking timbers still burning. Furniture and clothes littered the yard, and a woman was trying to get them into some sort of order. Three children worked with her, and a man was hunkered down beside the front wheel of a wagon, his head in his hands. The woman turned around as Burnett drove in, her face dark with soot and ashes and streaked with tears. There was a livid burn across her cheek. Burnett looped the reins about the brake and stepped down.

A small boy ran toward him. 'You leave us alone!' he yelled.

The woman shook her head numbly. 'Pay Joey no mind, Mr Burnett,' she said. 'He thinks you're one of them.'

Burnett's eyes shot about the yard. 'Them?'

'Ryan's men – Sheriff Mace, an' his deputy, Bob Oringer.'

Deems Bennett used the wheel of the wagon to pull himself erect. His voice was bitter as he said, 'You're a little late, Burnett, if you was thinkin' of doin' anythin' about it.' His bruised, bloody face twisted with pain.

'What happened?' Burnett asked.

Bennett laughed harshly. 'I held a patent on this land – at least I thought I did! Bought it nine years ago, free an' clear, but Mace had a paper said otherwise. An' he had a warrant for my arrest, too. Said I dynamited Three Waters last week, killin' forty head of his cows. Made it clear, damn him! I swallow that quitclaim deed, or get shot tryin' to escape arrest. Burned the house to make sure I left an' had nothin' to come back to.'

The woman stared about her. 'What's a man like Ryan want with what we got? We're less than the dirt under his boots.'

'We're in Lanyard County,' Bennett said, bitterly. 'This is God's land – and Jason Ryan is God.' He jerked erect. 'I never owned a gun, an' I wasn't choosin' sides agin' Ryan. Jay Miller come out here to see me, invitin' me to attend a meetin' they was havin' to try organizin' against Ryan's land grabs. I told him it was none of my affair.' Angry tears formed in his eyes, rolled down over his battered cheeks. 'I

111

ain't no coward. I don't like a takin' a beatin' from a bastard like Oringer an' not hittin' back. But I got a wife an' three kids. They gotta eat an' have a place to sleep an' clothes to wear. So I got to swaller it, pack my things an' get off land I bought honest.'

Burnett looked at the children. 'You got someplace to go?' The other shook his head wearily. Burnett nodded. 'My place is beyond the pass. You can stay there until you get your bearings.' He returned to his wagon, wheeled the team in a tight turn. He touched the brim of his hat to the woman as he passed her, then looked quickly away as he saw she was crying.

Hard, angry thoughts seethed in Pete Burnett's mind during the two-hour drive to Lanyard, but he kept them carefully under control. The hell of it was, Billy was partly to blame by giving Ryan an excuse to strike at men like Deems Bennett. And Billy, in his own way, would be as hard to stop as Ryan. Just the same ... Burnett's mouth thinned to a hard, straight line.

He was aware of a change in the town before he had ridden the length of the street. It was an intangible thing, compounded of a tightness in the faces of men he passed, and of openly worn guns on men he had never known to carry side arms. It was aggravated by the large number of Triangle riders in town, loafing along the boardwalk, arrogantly facing the street and all who walked upon it. In the clash of interests that had torn the valley apart, they had had all the best of it, and they wore the pride of tyrants as swaggeringly as they wore their tall hats. Burnett drove through Lanyard in silence. Even men he had known for years acknowledged him only by a curt nod of their heads. The tension was running taut, nearing breaking point, he thought soberly; a man was not accepted unless he was a part of the strife.

Burnett turned the team into Sutler's stables, and climbed down. Vance Sutler came up, carrying a pitchfork in one hand. 'Figgered you'd be back, Pete, sooner or later,' he said. 'Jay Miller wants to see you bad. Him an' the others hang around the Pine Tree. He's bunkin' at the Seeley House with Howie Richards. You'll find him one place or the other.'

Burnett frowned. 'All right, I'll see him. Then I want to rent a saddle horse. Might be gone two or three days. You keep the team for me.' Sutler nodded, and Burnett returned to the street.

The Pine Tree Saloon stood on the street below the Deadline. When Lanyard had enjoyed a brief silver-mining boom in the Torollones, the Pine Tree had been the fanciest place in town, but the years had done it little good. The heat seeping through the thin clapboard walls had discoloured the huge bar mirror, and the mahogany bar bore the scars of a thousand cow-town arguments. Burnett entered the place and saw Jay Miller at a table against the far wall. He was alone, and he stood up as Burnett came in.

Jay Miller was a rawboned man with sand-white hair and eyebrows, his high cheeks scratched with the red of a thousand tiny blood vessels. 'Been hopin' to see you, Burnett,' he said. 'We've had our differences, but trouble makes strange partners.' He held his voice low. 'You're thinkin' you've made it plain you see no sense in fightin' Jason Ryan on his own terms, so there's nothing I've got to say that will matter much. You're wrong, because I agree with you. You'll notice I'm packin' no hardware. I intend to give Ryan and his badge-totin' killer no excuse to gun me down. Now will you sit down and listen to me?'

Burnett hesitated, then pulled out a round-backed chair, spun it around, then straddled it. Miller held up his hand. 'Wally, bring us two beers.' He looked at Burnett. 'When I drink hard liquor I get mad, and I can't afford to now. I went to Swenson's funeral.'

He waited until the bartender brought two schooners of beer. His eyes were hard and intent. 'There's goin' to be hell in Lanyard County that will make what's happened up until now look like a Sunday school picnic. Ryan's backing every other rancher into a corner. He's used Billy Bascom's hell-raisin' as a sorry excuse to grab every spread that touches Triangle. He's gettin' away with it because he's covered, an' he knows it. He's filed claims that wouldn't fool a blind man, and Judge Mowery's approved every damned one of them. With Bob Oringer proddin' his butt, Jem Mace's done the dirty work. Three times men from Lanyard have tried to appeal to the Governor, but Carlisle's got both hands in

Ryan's pocket and ain't just about to pull them out. That makes it good, all the way up.'

Burnett sipped the warm, bitter beer and waited.

'I seen it,' Miller went on, slowly, 'and I made no fuss. I sent my family away, and I walked soft. But I've been to Santa Fe twice. The papers there know what's happenin', and they're ridin' Carlisle hard. He won't last long. You turn over a rock, and the vermin scurry like hell for cover. Carlisle's the dirtiest grub you ever seen. A petition, signed by fifty ranchers in this area, and backed by the newspaper, is layin' on President Hayes' desk this minute. I know for a fact he's telegraphed General Lew Walton, and that Walton's on his way to Washington tonight. You can bet your last nickel there's goin' to be some changes – and Ryan won't like them.' He drank his beer, studied the concentric rings the wet bottom of the glass had made on the scarred surface of the table. 'Ryan will fight to keep what he's grabbed. It will take time to lick him in court, but with Walton as governor, we'll get a fair shake. His first big job will be rootin' out the whole, dirty string of Ryan's toadies, startin' with Carlisle and endin' with Mace. I know Lew Walton, and he'll waste damned little time, but he'll need some help. We've got good laws in the Territory, but we're goin' to need good men to enforce them.' Miller met Burnett's eyes evenly. 'Men without a stake in this game. Men like you, Pete. I think I know how you stand on buckin' Ryan, but there's something else I'm not so sure of.'

Burnett frowned into his glass. 'You mean Billy?'

Miller nodded. 'Don't misunderstand me. I know what Billy's tryin' to do. But that doesn't make it right. A man like Ryan can twist the law to his own ends, but sooner or later it will straighten out. Billy Bascom's gone beyond any law, killin' Dorman the way he did. But maybe even that can be overlooked – if he stops now.'

'And if he won't?' Burnett asked quietly.

'Then the same law that strikes at Ryan will stop him.' Miller paused. 'I figgered I knew you, Pete. General Walton's got our recommendation for the man to replace Jem Mace. It's got your name on it.'

Burnett finished his beer and stood up. 'A man doesn't always

114

have a ready answer to a question. I haven't got one now. All I can say is, I'll do what I feel I have to do.'

Miller looked relieved. 'That's good enough, Pete.'

For a moment Burnett hesitated, then he turned and left the saloon. Busy with his own troubled thoughts, he returned to Vance Sutler's stables. He didn't notice Jem Mace following him with his eyes. Nor did he notice a few minutes later, as he rode out of Lanyard that the sheriff, mounted and waiting in an alleyway, followed carefully behind.

Firelight flickered against the grey, stone walls of Lost Creek Canyon, and shadows walked over the Indian signs painted on the rock. The seeping springs that had channelled one wall of the canyon were a never-ending source of water in a land so dry that a man could ride three days without finding enough to fill a canteen.

Hank Lewis had been studying the hieroglyphics for some time while he sipped a cup of black coffee. He motioned toward the wall of rock with the cup. 'Hell of a thing – all that writin' an' nobody able to read a single damned word of it.'

Jake Haley, given to spells of moroseness, spat to one side. 'Who the hell cares?'

Lewis ignored him. 'I as't a buck Injun once what that writin' was. You know that bugger didn't know? Said the Injuns made them signs was long gone before our Injuns ever showed up. Said he fig-gered they was news writin' – you know, like a newspaper, leavin' word from tribes passin' through what luck they been havin', how many kids the chief had, an' so on, to other tribes. Like a bulletin board on an army barracks wall. Wish I could read it. Been lookin' at them rock writin's for years, an' always wishin' I could read 'em.'

Haley snorted. 'What good it do you? If they been dead since before God knows when, who cares about their news?'

'I do,' Lewis said. 'I know I ain't never goin' to be able to read 'em, but it don't keep me from wishin' just the same.' He raised his head. 'You ever feel that way about somethin', Billy?'

Billy Bascom sat hunkered down, staring into the firelight. The past few weeks had thinned his face, made him look older than his years. Without lifting his head, he said, 'Too many things, Hank.'

Jake spat into the coals, and steam shot up. 'You figger we're getting' any place, Billy? I mean fightin' Ryan. I ain't belly-achin'—just wonderin'. It's beginnin' to look to me like we're three fleas on the backside of an elephant, and doin' about as much harm.'

Billy said, 'It takes time. One punch don't hurt much, but you keep getting' hit in the same place, an' pretty soon it gets tender, an' each little tap feels like a sledge hammer hitting you.'

Jake continued to scowl. 'Just the same, I can't help wonderin'.'

Hank Lewis moved closer to the fire. 'I been thinkin' about the same thing. Maybe it's like quittin' in the middle of a fight, but I can't see where we're doin' much. I keep thinkin' about Ryan, maybe layin' for him, getting' him in the sights of a Winchester – bang!' He snapped his fingers, the sound cutting into the quiet. 'That's it, the job's done.'

'No!' Billy's voice went brittle. 'I'm goin' to make him sweat. I'm goin' to make him crawl on his goddamn knees. He ain't goin' to have a chance, any more than he gave Trumbull, an' he's goin' to know it. It'll hurt when he gets it, because I'm goin' to step on him like I'd kill a toad.' He shook his head. 'I don't know how, an' I don't know when – but that's the way it's got to be. I guess it ain't right to make you two go along with my ideas. You can pull out whenever you're minded.'

'Hell, we savvy that,' Hank replied. 'Forget it. Fellers like me an' Jake ain't happy unless we're bitchin' about somethin'.'

The silence of the canyon closed them in, disturbed only by the soft mutter of the fire. Hank Lewis suddenly sat erect, holding up one hand. 'Somebody ridin' up the canyon!' he said. He moved swiftly, picking up a rifle and sliding down the slope toward the bend that concealed the firelight from the plains beyond. Jake faded from the circle of light, backing unhurriedly. Billy remained beside the fire. The soft, echoing clatter of a shod horse sounded closer, and a single horseman rode into the flickering firelight. Even as he rounded the bend, Lewis was behind him, rifle levelled. Then Hank's voice called out, 'It's OK – it's Pete!'

Burnett rode directly in and dismounted. He glanced around,

his long face solemn. 'You're takin' a chance, holin' up here,' he said.

'We ain't stayin long,' Billy replied. 'You joinin' us, Pete?'

Burnett shook his head. 'Nope. Figgered may you been out of touch. Ought to be filled in on some things.'

'That's obligin' of you, Pete,' Billy said. His eyes were wary, alert. 'You ridin' alone?'

'Turnin' in friends of mine ain't one of my failin's, kid,' Burnett replied. 'Although I could use the fifteen hundred bucks Ryan's offerin' for you.'

Billy's crooked smile went into place. 'Reckon I'm lucky. Ain't every man knows his own worth.'

'You could call it luck,' Burnett said. His sharp eyes took in their tattered clothes, their meagre camp, the fire-blackened frying pan that held their supper of salt pork and beans.

Hank Lewis grinned. 'It ain't that we're broke, Pete – we're just fussy about where we spend our money.'

Burnett didn't smile as he studied the three gaunt youths about the fire. 'It's been easy for you. Real easy. I don't know how you got that figgered, Billy; maybe you think you've got Ryan buffaloed, maybe you figger you're just a little too smart for him. Truth is, Ryan would double the reward to keep you alive. You're doin' him a real favour, kid. You're handin' him Lanyard County on a platter. Every time you take a lick at him, Ryan uses his bought law to grab what's closest to where you hit. He's makin' a show of "defending" himself against two-bit ranchers' thievery an' dirty tricks – an' swallowin' a chunk of Lanyard Valley every time. Maybe you know Deems Bennett – he's got a wife an' three kids. He's been run off his place, an' his wife an' kids are goin' to go hungry before he gets settled in again. All he had was that miserable spread, an' now Ryan's got it. But then Bennett's family is lucky – he's runnin' instead of fightin'. Carl Tait was killed "resisting" arrest for rustlin' you did, Billy. Charley Browner got sucked into a dust-up in town an' died in the street. Now a bunch of the others is standin' together. They'll make it a real shootin' war – an' that's just what Ryan wants. Most of the cause of it is you an' Jake an' Hank here. Course you've got

117

somethin' to show for it, Billy – you've pinned two tin badges to Harry Trumbull's grave marker. You figger it's worth it?'

Billy's face was hard in the firelight. 'We don't see it the same way, Pete.'

Burnett shook his head. 'Forget this crazy business, Billy. Quit now. It isn't too late. Jay Miller an' some others are takin' action that will stop Ryan. His toady, Governor Carlisle, will be out on his fat rump. President Hayes will appoint Lew Walton governor of the Territory. Walton will clean up this mess.' Burnett paused. 'I been asked to help him do it. The right way. If you keep on, you'll have to be stopped. I'd hate to have to do it.'

Billy took a step away, then turned back slowly. His face was drawn and tired. 'It sounds good, Pete. But I never was young enough to believe in Santa Claus. Sure, Walton can make Ryan pull in his horns, but by then, Ryan will have what he wants. He can tie it up in the courts so long everybody will forget what it's all about. You talk about them that's been hurt – all right, maybe Ryan's usin' me for an excuse. But if I stopped tonight, do you think Ryan would?' Billy's bitter laughter rang out. 'Maybe you figger we're just three two-bit cowhands raisin' hell. Jake said we're three fleas bitin' on the ass-end of an elephant. I don't see it like that. When we blew Three Waters, we killed maybe forty head of Triangle beef. That's what Ryan's thinkin', but what he don't know is there ain't been a drop of water there since. An' that means no water in a hundred square miles. Ryan's goin' to lose three thousand head of cattle on that range this summer. If he tried to get them off in a drive, we'll cover that country like a blanket. It's broken land there in the brakes, and his hundred men won't stand a chance. We'll burn every line shack, every stand of hay – then we'll fire the grass. Ryan's goin' to find the fleas takin' a chunk out of his hide that will make him limp. He can hire a thousand men, an' he can't cover Triangle. An' the bigger he makes it, the easier it'll be for us to tear it to pieces. Maybe your way is right, but there's too many ifs. I know what I'm doin', and Ryan will find that out. He may wind up ownin' all Lanyard County, but I promise you he'll find it nothin' but a wasted hell!'

Burnett sighed heavily and stood up. 'Then that's it,' he said, flatly. 'I'm sorry, Billy.'

'I am, too, Pete.' Billy stared into the fire. 'But it's a dirty job I figger somebody has to do.'

Burnett looked at Haley and Lewis. They exchanged glances, then Lewis said, 'I'm just sorry you're not ridin' our way, Pete.'

'Maybe I am, too,' Burnett replied. He hesitated. 'I'll leave some supplies cached out by Bennett's place. They'll see you through for a while.' He turned away, then swung back. His eyes met those of Billy Bascom for one lone moment, then he said, 'Good luck, kid.' He returned to his horse, stepped to the saddle. A few moments later his horse's hoofbeats faded down the canyon.

Concerned with their own thoughts, none of the three men spoke. Minutes passed, and then Jake grunted, bent to throw more greasewood on the fire. It smoked, then caught, blazed up brightly. He used his folded bandana to lift the coffeepot. He picked up his enamelled cup, started to pour coffee. He jerked suddenly, and the coffee spurted over Lewis' lap. Even as Lewis cursed and jumped back, blood gushed through Haley's flannel shirt. His face was shocked, numb. The shattering roar of a rifle racketed in the narrow canyon.

Haley's knees buckled and eyes glazed. Still holding the cup and coffeepot, he fell face forward into the fire. Lewis, cursing savagely, leaped to his feet, only to be smashed down by the second shot. Billy saw Haley's hair explode into crimson fury. His own legs drove him backward, and his revolver was in his fist, firing blindly into the night. Something struck his head like the slam of a hard-swung sledge, and in the burst of pain and shock, he didn't hear the third report of the rifle.

CHAPTER 11

Winston Carlisle looked about the big study and grimaced into his glass of brandy. Despite the money spent upon it, the room, like its builder, was without warmth. And somehow, the room and the man who dominated it had all but destroyed the angry determination that had brought him here. In the friendly confines of the old *palacio* in Santa Fe, he had felt self-assured, but now... His pasty face drew into hard lines, and he forced his voice into confident tones. 'It boils down to the simple fact you cannot ride roughshod where you please, Ryan, I'm afraid you don't realize the position you are placing me in....'

Jason Ryan looked across the wide desk. 'You've been paid,' he said, bluntly.

Carlisle avoided Ryan's sharp gaze. 'At the time we reached our – er – agreement, I did not understand just how far you intended to push this thing. A hundred thousand dollars is a great deal of money, but ...' His thick shoulders lifted in a shrug.

'You want more money.' Ryan stood up. His towering height and broad shoulders made him a giant looming over the short, squat governor. 'I want you to understand one thing. You've going to back me, every inch of the way. When I make a deal with a man, I live up to it – and he does, too. You've been paid, Carlisle. The deal is closed. Now you take your fat little butt back to Santa Fe and keep it there! If you try to shake me down for another dime, I guarantee you'll never live to spend it.' Ryan's voice was hard, brutal. 'Every minute, no matter where you are, I can reach you, Carlisle. Now get out of here.'

It was a badly shaken and soberly thoughtful man who arrived back at the capitol the next day. For the first time, Carlisle had taken a real look at this country and the men in it, and what he had seen had frightened him. Good God, did no man ever walk a street or ride a horse without a firearm of some sort within immediate reach?

His Mexican manservant bowed him into his quarters. 'There is a message, *Patrón*.'

A telegram stood against the quill pen in the stand on his desk. Impatiently, Carlisle crossed to the desk, picked up the yellow envelope and ripped it open. He read it, and his face paled. That damned idealistic fool Hayes had been reached! Carlisle's bright world was about to be crumbled about his ears, but a man learns to land on his feet. His thoughts were direct and fast. Ryan's hundred thousand dollars had been placed to his credit in a New Orleans bank. He could reach Chicago in a few days, and he had friends there who would discourage any pursuers. It would be simple to board a fast packet to New Orleans, and a few months of rest and pleasure. Slowly Carlisle began to breathe easier. That damned Ryan! Let him play his games with General Lew Walton. It would be like old Walton to call the bastard out – and kill him with one shot, too!

The governor was chuckling and finishing his third glass of good bourbon when he shouted for his manservant to pack his bags.

Jem Mace emptied his Winchester with the deliberate precision of an expert rifleman and reloaded without haste. In the canyon, one man had fallen across the blazing fire, and his body had smothered the flames. The depths were murky now, with only a few red gleams of light, but Jem Mace was sure enough of his marksmanship to know he had not missed with those first, three deadly shots. Taking his time, he levered shells into the chamber and fired, placing each shot carefully as he would on a target range. When the rifle was empty for the second time, the chance that any of the three men in the canyon were still alive was negligible.

The tenseness drained out of Mace's shoulders, and his lank form relaxed. The climb had been a hard one, taking him more than two hours, but once he had been sure where Burnett was riding, it had been a simple matter of getting there and waiting his chance. He had been tempted to drop Burnett, too, but the knowledge that he had Billy Bascom in his rifle sights had been too satisfying an emotion to hurry. He had traced the kid's every movement for ten minutes, enjoying the heady power of life and death, and Mace regretted only that Billy hadn't known of this last, grim joke.

Of course, Ryan would raise hell, but a man had to look out for himself, Mace thought, grimly. Now there would be time to breathe easy, to figure things out. Ryan was riding for a fall, and Mace was determined he would not go down with him. Overly ambitious men made things too complicated and wound up getting caught in their own machinations. To a man of Mace's blunt thinking, direct action was still best: never depend on anyone else, do your own dirty work, make sure it's done right, and forget it.

He peered again into the depths of the canyon. The last, red glow of the fire flickered dimly. He couldn't be sure of anything down there. He listened, holding his breath like an Indian; the silence was complete. It was unlikely that Burnett had heard the shots, but even if he rode back, Mace had nothing to fear. Rocks clattered some distance down the canyon; the sound echoed loudly. For an instant, alarm rang through Mace, and then he grinned. It wouldn't pay to jump at every noise, thinking that damn deadly kid was climbing out of the darkness, hunting for him silently. Mace enjoyed the chill that crept up his spine, and he actually chuckled to himself.

Just the same, he got up and shifted his position a hundred feet up the canyon, before hunkering down again. He looked east; the first, pinkish touch of dawn would be there soon. When there was light, he would make sure; meantime he would wait. Safe and sure, that was the way; any other way was damn foolishness.

Twice in the ensuing two hours, he changed position; and several times stiffened to the clatter of a fallen rock, only to force himself to relax. He chewed his cud of tobacco methodically, and carefully spread his drooping moustache to spit. He neither tired nor grew impatient. When the sky began to lighten, he got up, stretched, and considered the problem of getting down the steep cliff face. To go back the way he had come would take hours, and Mace begrudged them. He tugged at his moustache and spat again. A half-mile up the canyon were the remains of cliff dwellings and a trail that led from them into the canyon. Cradling his rifle in his arms, he left the rim and began the long, hard climb.

The canyon depths remained in the shadows, but the sky slowly deepened with red. Long strings of black clouds shot toward the far horizon. As the light grew he found it easier going, but just the same he was sweating by the time he reached the silent ruins sheltered by the overhanging, sheer rock cliff. Dark-eyed and ugly, they stared sightlessly down at him, and he hesitated. If Billy had survived the fusillade fired into the canyon he could be up there with a rifle, waiting. Mace forced the thought away quickly. There was no thrill to it now; a man got edgy sweating out the long hours of night. Mace turned his back on the ruins and started down the dim, worn trail. At the sharp edge of the precipice, there was a row of carefully balanced, giant rocks, the impregnable defence of people long since dust. Enemy attackers had faced tons of rock hurtled down upon them. Mace went past the first. Here the trail dropped to a ledge some eight feet below, and there were crude footholds gouged from the stone. He lowered his rifle, butt foremost, then swung over and dropped. He recovered his balance, stared down into the still-dark canyon before retrieving his rifle. The sunlight burst upon the huge rock towering over him, the weather-worn sides covered with painted designs probably intended to influence the fall of the balanced rock, to ensure its destruction of any enemy. Despite himself, thinking of that behemoth crashing down, Mace shuddered. He turned and started down. Suddenly he froze, every nerve, every muscle drawn tight.

Above and behind him, he heard a whispered call. 'Mace, look up!'

His arms were numb, and his body seemed to have no feeling at all, as Mace turned slowly back. A man stood above him, one lean leg braced against one giant, balanced rock, his back arched against another. The sunlight played full upon him, his bloody face and his torn clothes. It was Billy Bascom, smiling his crooked little smile, his eyes like bright blue flames.

'No!' Mace cried out. 'No, Billy, no!'

He tried to throw up the rifle, to jam himself against the face of the cliff, but it was as if he were immersed to the neck in mud, so slowly did his body respond. He saw Billy's lithe, slim figure bow, as leg and back went into his effort. He saw the grinding of the rock, shifting its weight. Little puffs of dust shot from beneath it. Then the rifle racketed; a white mark ripped across the face of the great boulder. Mace screamed with insane fear, and turned to run – but a man can't outrun tons of crushing, falling stone.

The resounding roar of the falling rock shook the very earth, and when Billy Bascom bent over the edge to look, the trail was empty, swept clean. From the canyon depths, dust filtered up, dancing in the hot, bright rays of the morning sun.

It took Billy an hour to work his way down to the heap of rubble and talus that marked the fall of rock. There had been places where the trail had been obliterated entirely. Here and there across naked rock were long, dark smears of blood and human flesh. He climbed over the fall at last. For a moment he saw nothing, then he made out a bony, broken hand, smashed and torn, thrust up starkly from the rubble. Billy worked his way across, bent and heaved broken rock away until he could reach Mace's body. He jerked the golden badge, bent and scratched, from the dead man's vest, and gripped it in his hand. Billy's face was dirty, and blood had caked upon it from a scalp wound. His light-hued hair was almost white with dust and shone in the bright sunlight. For a moment he balanced there. Then he pocketed the badge and moved slowly down the canyon.

Mid-afternoon of the second day after he had ridden out on his rented horse, Pete Burnett returned to Lanyard. He was tired and in need of a drink and a chance to sleep in a bed. He rode in from the north, and was halfway through the town before he grew aware of the hushed quiet. Puzzled, he reined in. The loafers' chairs on the front porch of the Seely House were vacant, and there wasn't a horse at any of the hitch rails that fronted the saloons. Most of the business establishments were shuttered, and shades were drawn over windows. He considered the town thoughtfully. A vagrant puff of wind spun dust devils at the far ends of the street, and a sheet of newspaper, caught in the gust, whirled through the air to rest against a clapboard building. Somewhere in the Mexican section to the south a dog was yapping. Otherwise the town was silent.

Disturbed, Burnett rode on slowly. He reached Vance Sutler's stables, and a round-eyed Mexican boy took the horse. 'Where's Vance? What's goin' on around here?'

The boy lifted bony shoulders in a shrug, his dark face blank. '¿Quién sabe?'

Frowning, Burnett said, 'I'll be back for my team and wagon in the morning. Tell Sutler I'll settle with him then.' The boy nodded, and watched him with expressionless eyes as he returned to the street.

The need of a drink, coupled with the harder need for information, sent Burnett through the swinging doors of the Pine Tree Saloon. He blinked in the gloom of the place, wrinkling his nose at the sour stench of stale beer and mouldy wood shavings that littered the floor. He walked to the bar, and the bartender grunted and motioned with a grimy thumb. Burnett followed the gesture, saw the raw-boned figure huddled across the table at the rear, head pillowed on arms, sand-white hair tousled and wild. The bartender set up a schooner of beer, and Burnett took it, drained it in silence. He set the empty glass down, then walked to the table.

'Miller,' he said. A boozy snort was his only reply, and Burnett kicked a table leg viciously, jarring the drunken man's head from his arms. It banged against the table, and he jerked erect, blinking angrily.

'Wha' the hell?' he demanded, then his eyes focused, and he shook his head. His wide mouth twisted bitterly. 'Pete, I tried to stop them – it was no good. Who the hell ever listens to a man who knuckled under once? That's what I did, knuckled under to that goddamn pig, Ryan, the dirty, rotten ...'

Burnett jerked out a chair and sat down. He gripped the rancher's arm hard, and the rambling curses stopped. 'What's happened?' he demanded.

Jay Miller made an effort to gather himself together. He gripped his head with both hands, and shook it savagely. Burnett motioned, and the bartender brought two beers. Miller lifted the glass, emptied it, then wiped foam from his mouth.

'This mornin', Pete,' Miller said, breathing hard. 'The goddamn fools wouldn't wait. Every damn small rancher in the valley – half the town, seventy-eight of them, all stirred up by Howie Richards spoutin' war talk, an' not a lick of sense in the whole lot.' Miller's haggard face moved brokenly. 'Hell, Pete, they were my friends. I tried to talk to them, make them understand ...'

'Where did they go?'

Miller blinked. Tears ran down his red-veined cheeks. 'I tried to tell them it was just what Ryan wanted them to do, goin' into Triangle after him – that he'd kill every damned one of them! But the stupid fools thought they was an army, an' nothin' could stop them. I got damned for a yellow-assed coward for tellin' them the plain truth.' He stopped and shook his head again. 'Hell, if they'd just waited a few hours....' He fumbled in his sweat-wet shirt, drew out a yellow telegraph form. 'The break we wanted, Pete. Carlisle's out on his fat behind, an' Hayes appointed Lew Walton governor of New Mexico this mornin'. It came two hours after they'd ridden out of town, too damn late to stop them or go after them.'

Burnett stood up abruptly.

Miller stared up at him. 'Where you goin', Pete?'

Burnett answered, 'I've been forty hours in the saddle. I'm goin' to bed.'

Miller fought to keep his blurry eyes focused. 'Then you'll be ridin' out?'

Pete Burnett's face was grim. 'There'll be dead men to bury, and somebody will have to stop Ryan killin' the rest of them, one at a time.'

'Sure,' Miller laughed brokenly. 'Only who's goin' to do it?'

Burnett stood very still. 'Me,' he answered, and walked away.

The land lay harsh and ugly in the light of mid-morning, shadows of the sparse outcroppings of soapweed and gram grass lay to the south, and dark-bottomed clouds were long, thin beads across the naked belly of heaven. These were the good months of the year, when the winds were cool, and the moistness of rain rode with them, and the grass greened up, and the anger of the land abated, gathering strength for the hot hell of summer. The land was patient, and the humid hush was like a long indrawn breath.

But the anger of the land was in the men, and they rode slowly together, and the raw, violent land waited.

Jason Ryan sat the stockman's saddle stiffly and erect. They had been there long minutes, and his huge, hard body had not tired; had showed no human weakness or emotion at all. This was a part of his pride. He was aware of Bob Oringer, hulking in his saddle, shifting restlessly, just as he was aware of the rest of his men; a long, straight line across the face of the land. Some were strong and waited with the patience of the professional fighter; others moved irritably, tiring, growing nervous. Jason Ryan marked each one in his mind. But nothing of his thoughts was permitted expression on the hard-stamped, hawk-like features – only solid, impassive strength.

This was the moment of truth toward which all of Jason Ryan's rugged life had pointed. Ruthlessly he had built his empire, founding it in bitter greed and strengthening it with hate of other men. So sure of this end had he been that he felt no elation, only a stolid acceptance that what he had taken by brutal force would after today be forever his.

Toward the silent, waiting line of Triangle men rode the second force, bunched together, driven by brooding resentment and sullen anger, but already raddled with doubts. Dust rose above them, and they rode in silence. The muted thunder of their horses' hoofs and the soft jingling of spurs were the only sound of their coming. The hard, flat light of the sun glistened along the oiled barrels of rifles dulled by a film of dust. It shone from the sweating, dirty faces of men who wore determination as a cloak for their fears.

They came together, two strong, angry forces. Their shadows puddled about the hoofs of their horses as the newcomers reined in, staring at the long line of mounted men who blocked their further passage. The pride of the strong marked one group, just as the other bore the stamp of righteousness. Both knew the final, bitter test was at hand.

Howie Richards was a man who would not have stood out in a crowd unless you saw his face. It was the bold, selfless face of a man who was dedicated to his own ideals and whom by his nature, could never compromise them. His voice, when you heard it, could shake your deepest convictions, and the seventy men who backed him now rode under his spell. He faced the cold, emotionless figure of Jason Ryan and let his horse walk forward a step or two.

'You have gone too far, Jason,' he said in his booming voice. 'You are not God Almighty to take as you please. Will you listen to reason?'

Jason Ryan might not have heard him for all the expression he showed. 'This is Triangle land,' he said, slowly, each word carrying clearly to every man present. 'Get off.'

And so strength met strength; and neither gave; and each was blind to the other. Howie Richards' belief in his own rightness could never be shaken. 'God forgive you, Jason,' he said in his bell-like voice – and reached for his holstered revolver.

Bob Oringer's single shot cracked with the angry sound of heat lightning, and Howie Richards stiffened in his saddle, then plunged to the earth. Before his body hit the ground, gunfire raged in a continuous tumult of sound. Horses reared and plunged, men cursed and screamed, and horses died and men died with them. Dust clogged the scene and rolled up in a yellow, ugly mushroom to blot the cloud-streaked sky. The unheard soughing of the wind was the angry land's sigh.

Jason Ryan sat still, his hard hand controlling his horse, keeping still the animal, which was more afraid of the devil upon its back than the hell that broke loose about it. He saw the long line of his men surge forward, the tension and waiting ended now, their faces gleaming with sweat and contorted with expressions of hate for those that faced them.

The hard core of Lanyard men melted, broke apart. They fought back, angrily, desperately, but there was no chance then, as there had been no chance before. One after another, riders toppled from horses and lay still, dust covering their fallen forms, making them crude, lumpish mockeries of men. The indignity of death was widespread, and touched the men of Triangle as well.

The thick, yellow dust bound them in. The racket of guns

128

lessened, swelled, then died into sporadic outbursts. Slowly the dust cleared, and Ryan saw the group of men who had faced him so boldly, broken and running. Then Bob Oringer's dirt-streaked face was grinning at him.

'Busted the bastards, by God!' he screamed, still in the frenzy of killing. 'They'll run and hide from their own shadows from here on in. Lanyard's yours!'

Ryan's face remained immobile, and his grey eyes regarded the terrible scene without expression. He rode forward to look down upon fallen men, then raised his head to look up and across the wide, barren land – his land.

Slowly a feeling of jubilance filled him, the greater because there was no doubt and no regret behind it. Without speaking, he turned his horse and rode toward Triangle. For once he did not drive the animal, but rode at ease in the saddle, proud arrogance subordinated to the gentler feeling of assurance; a man who has attained his greatest goal can afford to indulge in self-satisfaction.

He dismounted before his big house and looked off across the rolling plain. Greening grass rippled in a soft wind, like the low ground swell at sea, stretching away to the far horizon. Land, water, grass and cattle – these were the measure of a man's attainments, and from this day he would have no peers. He entered the coolness of the thick-walled house, his boots ringing on the polished tile floor. He went directly to his study and closed the doors behind him. For a long minute he stood before the map of Lanyard County, his face strangely alight. Then he moved to it and, with a sweep of his big hand, brushed aside all the red-topped pins. No need for boundary markers now!

He sank into his chair, whirling it so he could stare up at the big map. Minutes passed while he sat there, then he turned to his desk and lifted the square-faced whiskey bottle to pour a drink. The bottle was suspended over the shot glass when the huge window across the room exploded with a violent impact and something slammed into the wall behind Ryan's head. He heard the distant, muffled crack of a rifle repeated five times – almost a single, flat sound, and each time something struck the wall behind him.

Caught, for once, by complete surprise, Ryan poured whiskey that filled the glass, ran over and spilled across the wide, flat surface of the desk. The angry sounds died as abruptly as they had come, and he straightened the bottle and set it down. The big, plate glass window was broken, only sharp shards remaining in the frame. He wheeled slowly about to look at the wall above him. Across the big map of Lanyard County were five, evenly spaced bullet holes.

The double doors burst apart, and men ran in, pulling up to stare at him. Bob Oringer's big frame moved in.

'One man ... hid up there on the bluff. Goddamn, one of Richards' men couldn't have gotten through....'

'It was Billy Bascom,' Ryan said, slowly. For an instant, he wasn't aware he had spoken, nor was he aware of the odd high-pitched sound of his voice. When he realized, his face grew dark. 'Get out. Find him. Kill him!' He stared through the broken window. 'I'm offering ten thousand dollars for him, dead or alive.'

Men broke from the room in a rush. They left the double doors open behind them, and a Mexican servant closed them softly. Slowly Ryan became aware of the tremble of his big body. His face was wet with sweat. He looked up again at the pocked face of the map, and only then did he realize how carefully the shots had been placed. It would have been just as simple, if it had been the hidden rifleman's intent, to kill him with any one of them. The cold hand of fear touched him, and the jubilation, all the sense of triumph that had been his, turned to bitter emptiness. Until this moment, Billy Bascom had been nothing, a nuisance, a pawn to move in the exciting game of empire-building, but now ...

In this hard, brutal warning, Ryan read the meaning that Billy Bascom had intended it to have. The game was not played out....

Ryan lifted the whiskey glass. His hand had stopped shaking, but he felt the terrible, urgent need of a drink. Realizing it, he hurled the glass, untasted, from him to crash against the far wall. He stood up slowly, a savage, ruthless giant of a man. He moved to stand before the shattered window, defiant and erect. In that one terrible moment of shock and surprise he had weakened, and self-anger filled him. Ryan clenched one great hand, held it up.

'One of us!' he promised, viciously, and knew that this would be the final, greatest victory.

But the five, carefully spaced holes in the map were mockery of his might, and he knew vague, frightening doubts.

CHAPTER 12

The cantina of Enrique Noriega was crowded, and the low-ceilinged room was thick with smoke and the stench of wet wool and human sweat. Outside, the last warm rain of spring whispered against the puddle-pocked, muddy street. At the end of the room farthest from the bar, a Mexican wearing a silver-embroidered shirt worked lean, brown hands over the strings of a guitar, and a girl in a red-spangled dress danced, showing lengths of slim, dark-fleshed legs, while men hooted loudly and kept time by drumming the high heels of their boots against the hard clay floor.

The guitar made wild, clashing chords as Conchita spun around with her skirts lifted high and her black eyes contemptuously sweeping the faces of the men who stared so avidly at her. Like filthy animals – dogs lusting after a bitch in heat – she thought, bitterly. The exciting music swelled to a crescendo and stopped, and Conchita swept down gracefully. Men yelled their approval and applauded loudly, and silver coins rang out on the floor. A Mexican boy went down on hands and knees to gather them up.

Conchita came erect, hating the men, the cantina, the whole web of life that held her. She started for the door to the rear, then halted as a hand touched her bare arm. Bob Oringer grinned down at her and gestured toward a vacant chair at a table.

'How long has it been since you saw the kid?' he asked. 'Never mind – it's been long enough, but it will be longer still before you see him here in Lanyard.' His face hardened. 'Do you know where he is?'

Her laughter rang out. 'Who knows where the wind hides?'

131

Oringer shook his head, pulled a folded paper from his pocket. He took his time straightening it out, then turned it to face her.

WANTED, DEAD OR ALIVE, $10,000 REWARD.

'That help your memory any, baby?'

Conchita stood up, suddenly. 'I'm tired,' she said flatly. 'Leave me alone, Bob.'

His ugly face moved in a grin. 'Sure, baby,' he said. He folded the reward notice, thrust it into her hand. 'Just think it over.'

She stood there an instant, staring down into his eyes, then walked away. She passed through the door to the hall beyond and closed it behind her, leaning her weight tiredly against it. She could still hear the low, coarse mutter of men's voices and the clink of glasses on the bar, and she could still smell the harsh, feral stench of the cantina. Almost running, she fled to her room, closed and locked the door behind her. She went to the high window, thrust it open and stood there, letting the soft, warm rain blow in upon her.

Madre de Dios, how much longer could she remain the way she was, when her dreams were so bright, so clear, so real? She whirled about, and walked to her mirror, the spangles sending red slivers of light dancing up the drab walls of the room. She stood before it, staring at herself, and saw the crumpled paper in her hand. The new reward for Billy Bascom, $10,000.... She lifted her hand angrily, reached with the other and tore the notice in half and flung it from her.

She remained still, her eyes closed, her hands clenched. The soft patter of rain falling from the tiled eaves blended with the muffled noises of the cantina. A drunken voice yelled a curse that carried clearly through the intervening walls, and her slim figure shuddered. Slowly, then, hard lines moved into her face, and she opened her eyes. They found the two, torn pieces of paper on the floor and she moved quickly, picked them up, carried them to her dressing table. Her slim hands smoothed them out, joined them back together. Her bright-red lips whispered, 'Ten thousand dollars.'

Wind suddenly rattled the window sharply, and blew in rain that made a wet, dark stain across the dingy plaster wall.

The steadily turning vanes of the windmill made a threnodic shriek, rising and falling, as it worked the water pump. The last of the rains was a week past, and the shallow creeks and water holes were drying fast. Soon these tanks would be the only source of water for cattle in 400 square miles of grazing land. The shadow of the huge wooden tank beside the clapboard shack, dwarfing it, sprawled over the browning earth, and the man who lounged in the shade, a rifle across his lap, heard and saw nothing before a revolver barrel descended onto his skull with a sickening thud, and he fell senseless to the ground.

Billy Bascom straightened, gave the fallen man a cursory glance and studied the empty scene. He stood there, a worn, thin figure with nothing about him to suggest the half-legendary shape that filled so many columns of the Eastern newspapers. He was tired, dirty and hungry. And while he could not rest here, he could at least eat. He entered the shack, opened cans of food, ate his fill and dumped the rest of the supplies into a gunny sack that had served as a rug for the dirt floor. He toted this outside, then considered the towering height of the windmill and water tank. Frowning, he carried his food back to where he had left his horse, carefully scanning the horizon against the chance of being surprised. This was not likely, for he had watched the watering tanks for two days, and this morning a Triangle buckboard had come to drop off supplies and mail. Just the same, Billy remained alert.

The man he had buffaloed was stirring and groaning when Billy returned, and he unceremoniously dragged him by his boots into the shack and tied him with strips torn from a dirty pillowcase. That done, he went outside again. He searched for and found a heavy single-bit axe, carried it to the platform beneath the steel tower, and proceeded to smash the shaft and pump-housing into twisted wreckage. Sweating freely now, he circled the huge wood-sided tank. In places the sun-silvered staves were stained darkly with seeping water. Methodically taking his time, Billy chopped a hole, jumped back from the sudden, vicious flood of water that shot out thirty feet and flooded the dry sands. He watched until the water had emptied out and vanished into the sucking earth, leaving a long, ugly mud basin in the brown ground. After once again surveying the surrounding country, he turned his attention to the long row of watering troughs, smashing each one, watching it empty. The green-slimed bottoms began to brown in the glare of the afternoon sun.

Cattle were milling about the empty trough and starting to bawl as he rode out. There was no pleasure in his face for what he had done, and he did not look back.

Vance Sutler's face was compounded of red slabs of flesh carelessly placed over heavy bones, and anger didn't make him any prettier. He slammed a heavy shot glass on the bar of the Pine Tree Saloon, and snorted loudly. 'Two stinkin' months!' he said, harshly. 'And not one damned thing has changed. Ryan's still in the saddle, and with that goddamn wild kid chewin' on his behind, he's lettin' us know it.'

'It takes time,' Jay Miller interrupted. 'There's been no open fighting, and we've suits for legal action.'

'And Ryan's appealled every goddamn one of them!' Sutler exploded. 'I'm sayin' that maybe we could make Ryan listen to reason if Billy Bascom was stopped. I mean right now!'

Pete Burnett stood at the bar beside them. He glanced down at the silver star on his open vest, and frowned.

Jay Miller cut in quickly, 'Pete's doin' his job. Triangle hasn't hurrahed Lanyard since he's worn the star.'

'But will he bring in Billy Bascom? That's what I want to know.' Sutler's ugly features turned to Burnett.

'If I wouldn't, I wouldn't be wearing this star,' Burnett said, slowly. He finished his beer. 'Good night.'

On the street, Burnett paused in the cool darkness. The full heat of summer was two months away, but the nights were growing warm. He studied the street. The soft night sounds of the town buzzed steadily. Violence and hate seemed a million miles away on a night like this, but they weren't. They were close, pressing in upon the town, straining men's nerves taut, threatening to erupt in renewed fury.

The kingdom of the gun was a bitter kingdom, and without end, Burnett reflected grimly. Man against man, killing after killing, settling nothing, Perhaps the kid's way made sense, after all; at least it was something men like Ryan could understand and respect. For, in his own way, Ryan observed the rules, and had given Burnett no grounds for legal action. The hell of it was, the way it stood Ryan had won, for Burnett had little faith that the lawsuits would prove to be more than a waste of time; all the odds, as they had been from the beginning, were on Ryan's side. As for Vance Sutler's thought that stopping Billy would help to make Ryan listen to reason, Burnett held grave doubts that anything less than an ounce of lead in the right place would turn the trick. Which, Burnett decided half-angrily, was a hell of a way for an officer of the law to think.

A man came out of the Pine Tree, his boot heels echoing hollowly against the boardwalk. It was Jay Miller, and he approached Burnett. 'Sutler's like a lot of men, damn quick to yell about somethin' he hasn't the guts to do himself. It's true that Billy's goin' to have to be stopped – but bringin' him in isn't goin' to do one damn thing to soften up Ryan. Any damn fool can see that.'

'Sutler can't,' Burnett returned. He moved away, and Miller fell into step beside him. For a moment they were silent, then Miller struck a match to light a cigar.

'About Billy,' Miller said, slowly. 'I know how you feel about the kid. You're not the only one. Half the folks in this county would do him a turn if they could. I've talked to Lew Walton, and I can promise you he'll give the kid every break he can. A full pardon is not impossible – if Billy stops now.'

'Thanks, Jay,' Burnett replied. 'It makes what I have to do that much easier.'

Miller nodded and turned aside at the Seely House with a quick, 'Goodnight.'

Burnett crossed the street and walked back down toward the

courthouse. He went inside, down the dimly lighted hall, and started up the steps. The upper story was in darkness, and he frowned. The damn lazy janitor had forgotten to light the office lamps again. He climbed the steps slowly, felt for the low railing gate, pushed it open. By instinct he made his way toward his desk, found the lamp, raised the glass chimney, and then froze – every nerve strung taut.

Behind him the soft voice of a girl whispered, 'Do not light the lamp!'

Billy rode his horse at a walk through the belly-high grass that filled a narrow valley between two rolling hillocks. Cresting the western slope, he reined in and rolled a cigarette while he stared at the infinity of sun-browned, dry grass. His long, lean fingers shaped the cigarette. Then he licked the edge of the tissue, twisted the end and placed it between his lips. His eyes were narrow as he struck a match, lit the cigarette. For an instant he considered the burning matchstick thoughtfully, then bent from the saddle to drop it, still alight, to the ground. A thin wisp of smoke shot up and Billy backed the horse and waited. A circle of darker brown appeared on the earth, the smoke thickened to a column, and the tall grass seemed to melt away as the flames became invisible in the hot sunlight. The circle widened, and Billy wheeled the mare and rode once more toward the distant hills. He stopped once atop a rolling hummock to look back. Smoke, bluish-black, twisted across the sky, and against it the red of flames danced insanely to the push of the evening wind. Far out across the grasslands, the dots of running cattle were visible, scattering before the grass fire that would burn for miles before it would die.

Ryan's empire was compounded of four things: land, grass, cattle and water. Without grass or water, the cattle would die and only the land would remain. But a man grows up in this harsh land respecting the requirements for survival as he respects very little else; to destroy them deliberately was against every instinct. By fighting Ryan in this way, Billy was fighting something in himself. His hate had grown too great to control – Jason Ryan had become a symbol of all that Billy hated in himself, and by destroying the one, he would destroy the other.

It was dark when Billy turned his jaded horse into Hidden Valley Pass. The valley, on what had been Horn land, was isolated by the rough, jumbled rock of the brakes, and had once been used as a small horse ranch. There remained a crumbling adobe-wall building and corrals fenced with sapling bound together by rawhide thongs that had weathered iron-hard. There was grass and water – and small chance of discovery, which mattered more. Billy rode through the stand of pine that clogged the narrow entrance and pulled up sharply. Yellow lamplight spilled from the glassless window of the adobe hut, and a thin plume of smoke rose from the sod chimney.

Alarm shot through him and he covered the valley with his eyes. Only one strange horse was turned into the small corral behind the building. The ground was too hard to show hoof marks, and he could read no sign of any others. For a moment he held there, and then rode slowly forward, his rifle resting across his lap. He stopped the horse in front of the cabin, then the tension drained out of him, and he smiled at the slim shape of the girl who stood framed in the doorway.

She stood there, watching him from large, dark eyes, while he dismounted, unsaddled the horse and turned it into the corral. Walking slowly, he came toward her, and she backed away as he came into the single room. For one long, taut instant they stared into each other's eyes, and then she came into his arms and their lips met. Their hunger was mutual and not easily satisfied, and later, when she stirred from his arms and sat up, it was with reluctance.

'You must be starved, Billy,' she whispered, caressing his face with one slim hand. 'I brought food for you.'

He watched her and smoked a cigarette while she warmed food from cans and set a metal plate upon the warped board table. She poured coffee for both of them and kept her eyes upon his face while he ate. He did so in silence, with the steady appetite of a half-starved man, and when he finished at last, she refilled his cup. Her oval face remained impassive, and her silvery laughter, so much a part of her, was absent.

'What's wrong, *querida*?' he asked at last.

'Everything, Billito,' she replied, and a sudden, anxious expression broke the set of her features. 'You have done enough – too much....'

'Too much to stop now,' Billy cut in, soberly. 'Let's not talk about it.'

She shook her head, quickly. 'There will be no other time, Billy. That's why I came tonight. If I could find you, others can. But if we ride out now, tonight, we can be in El Paso in a day or two. My mother's family is in Chihuahua, and there you would be safe....' The set hardness of his face stopped her. 'You will not change, ever, will you, Billy?' Her soft voice filled with regret. 'All right, that is the way it must be, *no es verdad*? I will not come to you again – so tonight is all we will ever have.'

She came to him then, and the bitter-sweetness of their love filled them. With no future to build upon, both knew this moment must last forever, and with all the fire and strength of their youth, they gave themselves to each other.

'Wake up, Billy!' The softly spoken words penetrated the web of exhausted sleep, and Billy awakened suddenly. The grey light of dawn seeped through the open window, and against it stood the tall, erect figure of a man. It was Pete Burnett, and there was a revolver in his right hand and a silver star pinned to his open vest.

Conchita stood beside the rude table, her face pale, staring at him, and for a moment Billy lay there. Then he groaned and sat up. His mind was numbed with fatigue, and it was difficult to think clearly. Again he looked at Pete Burnett, and then toward the girl, and his face suddenly twisted with anger.

'You dirty little half-breed bitch!' The vile words came out flatly, and the girl bent beneath them as from the stroke of a rawhide whip. One long instant she stood there, her eyes deep, dark pools of misery and self-hate, and then she turned and ran from the room.

'She gave you a chance, kid. Why didn't you clear out with her last night? It would have been better like that.' Burnett paused.

'Just the same, by stoppin' you now before you raise more hell, she's doin' you the biggest favour anybody could.'

Billy's bitter laughter answered him. 'Sure, the two of you are! Thanks for killin' me, Pete.'

'You'll get a fair trial, Billy,' Burnett said, quietly. 'There are enough folks on your side to see to that.'

'With Bob Oringer still your deputy?' Billy laughed again.

Burnett frowned. 'I'll tell you what I told Oringer. I can't fire him, but I can sure as hell kill him.' He took a breath. 'Now get dressed – we're ridin' back to Lanyard.'

CHAPTER 13

Bob Oringer's lopsided grin was fixed to his ugly face as he lounged at ease in the big, white, rawhide chair. 'So Burnett brings in the kid. I seen him in his cell an' felt like spittin' in his face.' Oringer sobered. 'The hell of it is, he ain't goin' to stay there. Miller an' Burnett have it all worked out. The kid will be tried in Lanyard, an' you know damn well there ain't twelve men in that stinkin' town will vote to hang him. They'll slap him on the wrist for disturbin' the peace or somethin' – an' Governor Walton will have his pardon all made out an' signed.'

Jason Ryan swung his heavy chair back to look up at the five bullet holes that pocked the big county map. 'You'll see that Billy Bascom doesn't stay in his cell until time for the trial.'

Oringer stiffened. 'Damn it to hell, Jason, you want him on the loose again? Ain't he all but wrecked this goddamn ranch? Give him enough time an' you'll find yourself ownin' nothin' but barren land.'

Ryan turned slowly to face the other. 'No, Billy's outlived his usefulness,' he answered. 'The Lanyard County War has ended.'

'Then what the hell …' Oringer broke off in mid-sentence and frowned. 'I get you, an' I wouldn't need no urgin' if it wasn't for that damned Burnett. I make a move, an' he'll shoot first an' worry later. I know you worked it for me to stay on as deputy, but I won't be a hell of a lot of use to you buried on Cemetery Hill.'

'Billy Bascom alive and Billy Bascom dead are two different things,' Ryan interrupted. 'You'll find that people worry about things that might happen, but damned little about something that's over and done with. I want you to ride back to town and stay there. You'll know when to do what I want you to. Take no chances, and make it look good. The kid can be expected to make his try – nobody will be surprised.'

Oringer stood up, walked to the door, then hesitated. 'Sure, but what about Burnett?'

'I haven't forgotten Pete,' Ryan answered grimly. 'Don't get overanxious, Bob. You'll be sheriff of Lanyard County for a long time.' He turned again to look up at the bullet-marked map. His cold, hard voice stopped Oringer at the door. 'One more thing. When Billy's dead, I want you to bring me one of his ears. I'm going to nail it to that map.'

Billy Bascom lay back on the hard bunk, his hands pillowing his head, but his eyes were open. The approaching thud of booted feet caused him to sit up on the edge of the bunk. Bob Oringer's hulking shape came down the corridor, and the big man stopped in front of Billy's cell.

'Got news for you, kid,' Oringer said. His malicious grin warped his thick mouth. 'But you ain't goin' to like it. Your pal Burnett just rode out of town. He thinks he'll be back in a couple of hours, but I know better.' Oringer laughed, then broke off. 'You got too many friends, kid, so we're eliminatin' one of them today – an' you along with him! But first we're changin' some things. We want you to be comfortable.' He raised his voice, 'Gryson, bring those chains in here!'

Another deputy came in, scowling. 'Look, Bob, Burnett's goin' to raise hell about this!'

'Not where he's goin'!' Oringer guffawed loudly. He took the leg and wrist irons from the other man. 'Cover the little bastard – if he so much as blinks, kill him!'

Gryson nodded and drew his revolver as Oringer unlocked the cell door. Billy came to his feet only to stagger back against one wall under the smashing impact of Oringer's fist. Blood trickled out of one corner of his mouth. Oringer moved in quickly, swung the heavy leg irons in a short, vicious blow that dropped Billy half-conscious to the floor. He felt Oringer's hard hands grip him, then the bite of the wrist irons, followed by the leg clamps. A short length of heavy chain bound the two together so he could not raise his arms higher than his chest. Oringer was sweating hard when he finished and stepped back to swing his booted foot in a hard kick. Billy groaned and fell on his side while Oringer's brutal laughter rang out.

He bent, jerked Billy to his feet by one arm, and dragged him into the corridor. Billy staggered, almost fell, and Oringer slapped him viciously. In the office, he thrust him into a chair, then bent over him.

'I've waited for this a long time,' he whispered, hoarsely. 'A goddamn long time. I'm goin' to make it count. I'm not goin' to end it quick for you – but I'm goin' to make you wish to hell I had!'

He locked his blunt fingers in Billy's hair and struck short, hard blows that smashed flesh and cartilage. Only when Billy's head dropped forward to his chest did Oringer step back, breathing faster, his eyes insane. He crossed to Burnett's desk, dumped water from a pitcher into a glass and drank deeply. He carried the pitcher back and dumped the water into Billy's bloody face. Billy shook his head and raised it, his eyes still glazed.

'God, Bob, you'll kill him!' Gryson protested.

'You're goddamned right I will!' Oringer returned. He was held there in the grip of his own brutal passion, then licked at his thick lips. 'But first there's something important.' He turned to Billy. 'You know what Ryan wants, kid? One of your ears. He's goin' to nail it to his wall to remember you by, just like he'd take the hide of a lobo wolf. An' come to think of it, there ain't no better time to oblige him than right now.'

Still grinning, he dug into his pocket, brought out a jackknife, opened the long, shiny blade, and held it up in front of Billy's eyes. 'Maybe I'll cut the other one off, too, an' send it to Conchita for a souvenir.'

He moved forward. Billy tried to come out of the chair, but Oringer was too strong and too fast. One clubbing blow knocked Billy back, and then Oringer's weight pressed him down, holding him still. He felt Oringer's hot, whiskey-stinking breath on his face; the one iron-hard hand gripped his head like a vice. Insane, burning pain shot through the side of Billy's face, and a scream tore through his clenched teeth. Then his body went slack.

Oringer stepped back, his hands and knife bloody. He spat to the floor. Gryson had turned away and was standing beside the door that opened onto the balcony that overlooked the street. Oringer pulled his bandana from his pocket, wiped his hands and knife, then put his grisly prize into the bandana, folded it and thrust it back into his pocket. He looked at the bloody figure in the chair, then spat once more to the floor.

'Keep an eye on him, damn you!' he ordered, angrily. 'I want him awake when I kill him. I'm dry. I'm goin' across the street for a drink. I'll finish the job when I get back.'

Pete Burnett studied the boy who rode beside him, and frowned. Jeb Lee's son was not over fourteen, and despite his efforts to conceal it, his face betrayed more furtiveness than anxiety or fear. When he had come into town with the story that his father had been shot, Burnett was too accustomed to trouble to give it much thought, but now, two hours out of town, he had time to think, and he was beginning to worry.

'You say they rode in this mornin', shot your pa an' rode back out again?'

'I told you what I know,' the boy answered, sullenly. He avoided Burnett's eyes.

Urging his horse to a faster pace, Burnett looked around. The land was still and hushed. The morning sun was hot and bight, and black shadows streaked the grasslands, marking hummocks. The Lee place occupied a triple-section north of Triangle, beyond the

broken land of the brakes and of little value to Ryan. Perhaps for
that reason, Lee had not shared in the troubles of Lanyard County
– until now, Burnett corrected himself. The boy rode in silence
a little behind Burnett, as if to avoid further conversation, and
Burnett did not press him. The frown between his brows deepened,
however, and his mouth remained a hard, tight line. They reached
the turnoff, and Burnett rode down the wagon-rutted trail. They
passed a broken, split rail fence, and as the sod hut came into sight
the boy turned aside. 'You ride in with me!' Burnett called out
sharply.

The boy's quick stare was almost frightened, but he wheeled
his horse after Burnett's. They rode into the yard together, and
the boy's nervousness worsened. He reined in, and Burnett pulled
up his horse shortly. The boy, suddenly gripped by open fright,
tumbled from his horse and began to run, his short, brown legs
churning in the dirt of the yard. Instinctively, Burnett reacted,
coming off his mount in a single lunge even as a rifle barked thun-
derously. He hit the dirt, running hard, his revolver in his hand.
He saw the rifle barrel protruding from the glassless window of the
shack, and snapped three quick shots as he ran. A man screamed
with pain, and something crashed inside the shack.

Burnett hit the plank door at a run, struck it heavily with one
foot, and burst it inward. He was inside before the two men at the
window could swing toward him. One man was gripping his side,
his face stricken. The other tried to fire his revolver, but Burnett's
shot caught him in the stomach, dumped him to the floor. The
man still standing suddenly fell, his staring eyes glazed in death.
The stench of black powder smoke was strong as Burnett stared at
the two dead men. He had never seen either one of them before.
He stood still, breathing hard, then slowly ejected the empty shells
from his revolver and replaced them from his gun belt. He holstered the weapon, then stepped back through the door to the
sunlight.

'Lee!' he yelled. 'Come out, or I'll burn this stinkin' hovel to
the ground!'

'All right, Sheriff!' a man's voice called, and Burnett wheeled toward the roof-sagging barn at the far end of the yard. Jeb Lee came out slowly, a pot-bellied, beard-stubbled figure, both hands up in the air. 'Hell, Pete, I couldn't warn you …'

Burnett's raw anger burned inside him and he cut the man off. 'Talk, goddamn you – loud an' clear, or I'll break every bone in your rotten body!'

Jeb Lee's tobacco-juice stained mouth quivered. 'I didn't do nothin',' he whined. 'A man's got to live, Pete. They rode in here, threatenin' to kill me. I had to send the boy …'

Behind Jeb Lee, the boy edged closer, white-faced and frightened – and ashamed. 'Pa ain't got no guts at all,' he said, bitterly. 'I didn't want to come after you, but Pa said they'd kill him if I didn't, an' with Ma sick over Heckelman's …' He fought back tears, swallowed heavily. 'I heard them talkin' about it, how they would get you out of town so Bob Oringer could get at Billy Bascom. Honest, I didn't know they was goin' to try to kill you!'

Burnett stiffened. 'Listen to me, Jeb!' he bit out. 'If you ever mix your kid into dirty business like this again, I'll kill you, so help me God!' Then he spun on his heel, ran for his horse. As he sent the animal racing back the way he had come, his face was dark and strained.

Raw, merciless agony brought Billy to his senses. He raised his head slowly, his whole face alive with pain. Through bleary, bloodshot eyes he saw Gryson watching him. He strained to sit erect, forced himself to stand free of the chair.

'Don't try nothin', kid!' Gryson said, warningly, a bared Colt in hand.

The bitter, salty taste of blood was in Billy's mouth, and he spat to clear it before he tried to speak. His voice was a hoarse, unintelligible rasping sound. He tried again, and the word came out, whisper-soft, 'Favour …'

Gryson moved closer, warily. 'Get back in that chair!'

Billy shook his head, and blood dripped down his neck, soaking his ragged shirt. 'Do … me … a favour,' he murmured through battered, swollen lips. His manacled hands dug into his waistband,

and he held out a thick, golden coin. He saw interest grow in Gryson's eyes as the deputy came nearer. 'It's yours – for a favour,' Billy managed to say.

Gryson hesitated, greed and caution fighting each other. 'Doin' what?'

'Just … Just a message … to my girl,' Billy mumbled, and held out the coin.

Gryson was directly in front of him. 'I don't know, kid. Hell, Oringer'd kill me.' He licked at his mouth. 'What the hell? A man deserves a favour before …' He grimaced. 'What do you want me to tell her?'

'Tell her …' Billy shivered suddenly with pain, and the coin slipped from his hand, rang out against the planked floor.

Gryson bent forward, reaching for the fallen coin. His head came down level with Billy's waist – and instantly Billy's manacled arms shot up and then down in a vicious, chopping blow that knocked Gryson to the floor. Billy went down with him, striking with insane deadly fury, again and again, until Gryson's features were broken, bloody ruins. He lay prone on the floor, moaning, and Billy kicked him savagely in the head, then bent to pick up his fallen Colt. He thrust it into his waistband, then darted a quick glance about the room. He saw a glass-fronted cabinet that held rifles and shotguns, and smashed it with a swing of his arm chains. He drew forth a double-barrelled weapon and broke it. His hands, slippery with blood, fought to shove shells into the chambers. They slid home, and he closed the gun with a snap. Carrying it, he jumped, feet together, toward the door that opened onto the balcony. He reached it and sagged there, staring down into the sun-baked street.

His wait was not a long one. Across the street, Bob Oringer came out of the Pine Tree Saloon. He swaggered to the edge of the boardwalk and held there, brutal arrogance stamped on his face. For a long moment he remained there, staring up and down the street, feeling his power over the town, glorying in it. He didn't look up at the balcony of the courthouse as he started across the street.

Billy stepped through the doorway onto the balcony. He walked stiffly, almost blindly. The street seemed to waver and dance in front of him, and only Oringer's tall thick figure was real. It seemed he had never before seen anything so clearly; he could make out the dark sweat circles under Oringer's arms, the stubble of beard on his cheeks, the rime of sweat salt and dust at the base of the brim of his Stetson. Billy's crooked little smile painfully moved his blood-streaked features, and he raised the shotgun, held it steady.

'Hello, Bob!'

Bob Oringer halted in the centre of the street. His red face went white, and his belly seemed to bulge and sag. His jaw dropped open, and his eyes stared up. He tried to force his body to move, to jump to one side, anything....

Billy pulled both triggers of the shotgun at the same time, and the recoil slammed him backward, almost knocked him off his feet. He forced himself to stay erect, to stare down. Both charges struck Oringer fairly in the centre of his body, and they tore his clothes to shreds and his body to lead-churned pulp. He was dead before he fell, and when he did fall, it was slackly, as if every tendon in his body had been severed at the same instant. Beneath him the dust of the street turned to red mud.

Men ran from stores and saloons, stared at the fallen Oringer, and looked up at the terrible, bloody figure on the balcony, but none spoke, none ran into the street. For an instant Billy remained there, then he hobbled back inside. He found his hat and gun belt and gun. He buckled on the belt, loaded his revolver and then went slowly down the stairs. In the foyer three or four silent, wide-eyed men watched him as he passed them. He reached the street, looked once toward Oringer's huddled shape and then surveyed the town. Nothing moved; people seemed frozen where they stood. There was no menace, no emotion of any kind in their detached bearing. Billy moved with his hobbled gait out to Oringer, bent and tore the shot-dented badge from his chest then straightened slowly. Nothing had changed; it seemed as if this moment had been caught in an eddy of the time stream and would never pass.

Billy made his way down the centre of the street, and the watchers followed him with their eyes. He reached the blacksmith's shop, and the steady ring of the hammer did not pause as the man bent over the anvil looked up. The soot-blackened face was expressionless. Billy went in, held out his manacled arms.

The blacksmith met his eyes evenly, then winked and pulled a cold chisel from its holder. He bent to the task, and the heavy hammer and the sharp blade cut the manacles quickly. A second sledge served as a base to cut the leg irons, and Billy stood free.

'What do I owe you, Jim?' Billy asked.

'Not one damned dime,' the blacksmith answered. He shifted a quid of tobacco from one cheek to the other, then spat into the glowing coals of the hearth. 'I ain't never seen you in my life.' He bent, picked up the broken irons, tossed them into a refuse barrel, then returned to the bellows and did not look up as Billy went out.

A small, dark-skinned man stepped from the boardwalk toward Billy. 'You'd better let me fix that ear,' he said. His eyes met Billy's levelly. 'No one in this town will try to stop you, nor see which way you ride when you leave.'

Billy nodded, tried to smile his thanks, reeled dizzily and would have fallen if the doctor's strong hand had not gripped his arm. He was helped to an adobe structure set back from the street. The doctor spoke to a Mexican who stood in front of the building. 'Get his horse, *hombre!*' The man jumped to obey, and Billy was led into the office.

He sank into a chair, and the doctor's light touch probed at his head. 'Men are the filthiest of beasts, and Bob Oringer the dirtiest pig of all. The cut is clean – but your ear is gone.'

Iodine burned fiercely, and pain wracked Billy, and he was almost sick. Then the fire lessened, and the soft bandages were wrapped around his head. He stood up at last.

'Men always fear those who will not back down, those who strike back when they are struck,' the doctor said sadly. 'They will not openly condone what these other, these violent ones do – but they never forget them.' He sighed. 'Goodbye, Billy!' He held open the door, and watched as Billy went back into the hot sunlight and climbed wearily into the saddle.

The street remained still and silent, and Oringer's broken body still lay in the dirt. Billy didn't look down as he rode past. He came to the Deadline, passed it and rode on until he reached Enrique Noriega's cantina. Here he pulled up and swung down. His face was white, and the bandage about his head was already marked with seeping blood. He walked through the open doors into the dark interior, and the soft twanging of a guitar stilled, the last low note vibrating on the silence of the room.

Two or three Mexicans were at a table at the back, and the guitar player sat in a back-tilted chair, a cigarillo adroop between his lips. His black eyes fixed to Billy's face.

Splintered light from bright-red spangles danced about the room, and Billy halted. Conchita came toward him slowly, her slender form in the shining dress like a dull flame in the shadowed cantina. Her oval face was pale and set, her eyes wide, dark night pools. 'I knew you would come,' she whispered.

Billy's right hand moved, and his long, thin-bladed knife appeared from his waist. He held it before him, and the girl stood still, her eyes half-closed. 'Kill me, Billy,' she whispered, her voice like the soft murmur of the wind. 'As I killed the dream I tried to make come true. I want so much, so many things – and too late I discovered you were all of them....'

Billy remained still. One swift movement of his hand, and he would even the score as he always had. One swift slash, and there would be no more hate for her inside him. One hard, sure stroke, and she would fall, and a half-breed girl who had never had a chance could be forgotten....

'Goodbye, Conchita,' Billy said, then bent swiftly forward, and brushed his lips across her cheek. He backed hurriedly, and was gone. Only then did the girl begin to weep.

The early-afternoon sun sent the shadow of the wooden cross downward across Harry Trumbull's grave. Billy stared at the three badges fastened to the wood, then bent and shoved the pin of the fourth into the crossbar. He straightened slowly, his face white and terrible.

'There is just one more, Mr Trumbull,' he said gently. 'Just one.'

CHAPTER 14

Fiesta time had cone again to Santa Fe, the Royal City, and the plaza had been turned into a carnival ground. Native and Indian markets abounded, and the gala news was that General and Mrs Ulysses S. Grant had come to see the sights of the holiday. The solemn march to the Cross of the Martyrs had taken place, and the re-enactment of the historical reconquest by de Vargas had been a tremendously successful pageant. The town was alive with carnival spirit, and strolling musicians and bands competed with one another. Whole streets writhed with gaily dressed dancers. And tonight was the Governor's *baille*, with General Grant and his wife as guests of honour. There would be great bonfires in the street to celebrate the ending of the fiesta.

Through the half-opened French doors of his study, the gay sounds of the town came indistinctly to Governor Lew Walton as he sat at his broad desk writing slowly and methodically with a quill pen. He was a big man, still hard and muscular, with the far-away look of a dreamer about his eyes. Only the heavy jut of his chin belied it, though the fist that held the pen was just as familiar with leather reins and the stock of a rifle. A final thought expressed on paper, Lew Walton chewed of the tattered end of the quill and frowned at the leather-backed books that sat in a row atop the desk.

It was early evening, and the single student lamp on his desk was the only light in the shadowy room. A string of firecrackers went off in the distance, and a faint smile curved Lew Walton's broad mouth. He had dressed earlier and, except for the well-worn silk smoking jacket he wore, was ready for the ball. It was the first major function in this newest turn his brilliant career had taken, and he was looking forward to it. God knew that Carlisle had left him enough problems – it was time he had some fun! He leaned back in the big chair, then tensed as he sensed the presence of someone near him.

'Who is it?' he demanded sharply, turning his swivel chair.

A lithe form stepped out of the shadows near the French doors and moved toward him. The lamplight shone first upon the ugly, black barrel of a revolver, and then upon a thin, boyish face that bore a twisted smile that revealed prominent white teeth.

'Just me, Governor,' the boy said. 'The gun is just for quiet. I keep hearin' you want to talk to me. I always like to oblige a man when I can. I'm Billy Bascom.'

Lew Walton's face registered surprise. 'The hell you are!' his hard, read voice exploded. 'By God, you've got your nerve.'

'And my gun,' Billy reminded him, softly. 'Lower you voice.'

For a moment resentful anger stirred in Lew Walton, and then, despite himself, he laughed. 'I should tell you to go to hell,' he said. 'But I admire your manner – or lack of same. Come in, Billy. Point the gun some other way. I haven't yelled for help yet, and I'm too old to begin now.'

Billy's quick, hard gaze measured the big man, then he nodded and reholstered the revolver. He came to stand in front of the desk, and his eyes read the titles of the books, and his smile widened. 'I'm sorry to bust in like this, but you did the invitin', and with so many people in town I figgered I had a chance to ride in unseen. I won't get another, so I'll have to ask you to put it plain – and quick-like, because I ain't got much time.'

Lew Walton studied the boy, and shook his head. 'You're not as young as I've heard – but younger than I thought you'd be.' He frowned. Despite the romantic stories that had built this incredible young man into a legend, he had expected coarse brutality to be a part of him, but Billy's features were fine and regular, and his smile was that of a normal boy. 'Your head ...' He hesitated, frowning harder.

'Bob Oringer took an ear,' Billy said. 'I took something in return he valued a hell of a lot more.'

The Governor looked down at his desk. Several times he had toyed with the idea of meeting the boy outlaw, and he had worked out some nicely moral speeches to fit the occasion. The dramatic appeal of such an event had aroused his creative writer's instinct, and he had thought of a thousand questions – and not one of them seemed suitable now. He shook his head slowly. 'If you were indifferent to what you've done, if you were proud of it, or even ashamed, I'd know what to say to you, Billy,' Walton mused. 'But I'm not sure that you are any of these things.'

'If you mean, did I like doin' what I've done – I didn't.' Billy's smile was gone. He looked younger, almost innocent, and far too tired. 'If you mean, do I think I've done somethin' fine and proud – I don't. It was mean and dirty and low – but not as bad as what Ryan's done.' He paused. 'I'm not ashamed of doin' it, but I'm ashamed of havin' to – if that makes sense to you.'

Walton met his eyes, then nodded, resignedly. 'I'm sorry to say it does.' He sighed heavily and leaned back in his chair. His eyes were penetrating, and – Billy thought – he'd be one hell of a hard man to lie to. 'But I find myself more interested in you than in what you've done,' the Governor went on. 'I suppose you realize you've gone as far as you can go? What's past won't be forgotten – but its importance will diminish.'

'It's just as true about what Ryan's done,' Billy put in, softly.

Reluctantly, Walton nodded. 'I'm afraid it is.' He raised his head, and his heavy jaw was set and firm. 'Just the same, I must warn you, you can do no more and expect it to be forgiven. Do you understand me? If you surrender now – tonight, to me – I will bend every effort in my power to see that you are treated justly. This does not mean a free pardon. You will be tried by an honest court. I believe I can assure you that their finding will be tempered with mercy. It may mean prison for you – it's almost certain to – but you will still be a young man when you are released, and you will be free.'

'And what happens to Ryan if I quit now?'

Walton met Billy's eyes levelly. 'I won't lie to you. Ryan has worked very carefully, screening everything he has done behind a cloak of false legality. It has fooled no one, and I don't think he expected it to. But legally he can't be touched. There will be court actions against him, and some may be won, but not many. It costs money to fight legal battles, and only Ryan has the ammunition for a long war.' He paused. 'Few things are just and fair in this life, Billy, but we can't go around trying to right the world's wrongs by committing more.'

Billy nodded, his smile returning. 'Thanks for the straight talk. I believe you, Governor.'

Walton looked up quickly. 'Then you will surrender – end this crazy war you have been fighting?'

Billy backed to the edge of the circle of lamplight. 'No,' he said, flatly. 'I can't.' One lean hand gestured toward the books atop Lew Walton's desk. 'Every man likes to leave somethin' behind him. Maybe it's just pride, I don't know. But it's somethin' real. You just said the world ain't fair and just – but you write big, thick books tellin' stories about the times of Christ, and makin' up parables and morals, and tryin' in your own way to balance out the good and evil. That's the mark you're leavin' behind you, and it will stand a long time. I ain't much at writin', but I'm goin' to balance out the scales a little myself, this once, and I'll be remembered, too – even if it's just for the number of men I've killed.'

The boy's face hardened to that of a man, sharp and strong. The blue eyes were cold and deadly. For an instant Billy Bascom held there, and then he was gone, and his whispered, 'Goodbye, Governor!' still echoed in the room.

Lew Walton remained still a moment, then came out of the chair in a bound. The damned, young, contrary pup! A call to his guards, and there wouldn't be a chance of Billy Bascom riding out of Santa Fe! He reached the pull cord at the door, grasped it, then relaxed his hold without pulling it. Slowly the irritated lines faded from his face. He released the cord and walked slowly back to his desk. He resumed his chair, and his solemn eyes studied the spines of his books. A man's mark against the flow of eternity.... He took pride in his writings, and felt it now. But there was another kind of pride, and another kind of mark to make. The printed word or the legend? Which would last the longer?

Through the crowded streets of Santa Fe, thronged with merrymakers, rode Triangle, a solid, proud army of mounted men. Well dressed and well armed, they rode as the victors they were, aware of the attention they received and savouring it as their just due. Flankers rode ahead and to each side of Jason Ryan, eyes wary and sharp, rifles ready to hand. People made way for them, and the merry voice of the crowd died with their coming and took time to resume in their wake.

Ryan had taken Lanyard County, and it would remain his. There was no power on earth to seize back what he had taken, and the knowledge was a heady thing, as strong as good whiskey. Ryan rode erect in the saddle, his rock-like face expressionless, but his eyes glowing. There were still problems, but, except for Billy Bascom, they counted the reward to twenty thousand dollars, the largest in the history of the Territory. Such was his faith in the power of money that he accepted Billy's death as an accomplished fact. So it was with a free mind he had ridden here tonight, and despite the fact that General Grant would be present at the great *baille*, Ryan knew where the centre of attention would lie. So occupied was Ryan with this pleasant thought, the faces of the crowd were blank white masks to him, and he did not notice the slender youth who drew back into the shelter of a doorway as the Triangle group passed down the street....

Billy sensed something of the jubilation behind Ryan's impassive face, and his arm ached to draw his revolver, to send a leaden slug smashing into that arrogant rocklike mask. Not yet! he whispered fiercely to himself, and pressed the hard, round stick thrust into his waistband. The last of Triangle rode on, and Billy left the doorway, pushed through the crowd to the street. Laughter and noise racketed around him as he forced his way in the wake of the riders.

In the centre of the plaza, a great heap of boxes, barrels and crates had been built, and men carrying torches stood nearby, grinning, as latecomers scurried forward with their wooden fire-offerings.

'Hurry it up!' A man yelled, excitedly. 'We'll be touchin' her off in a minute! Yessir, we're really goin' to have a bonfire!!'

Billy paused. A man jarred him, pushing past with an empty box. Billy's smile twisted his mouth grimly. He needed a diversion, and this was made to order. When the fire was ignited, people would draw back to a safe distance, and a stick of dynamite buried deeply would hurl flaming wood over half the town. *And the time it would take for the fire to reach the fuse would be enough....*

Billy moved on, fighting his way through the crowd toward the *palacio.*

Triangle riders cleared passage across the crowded plaza, and fanned out before the gay, lantern-lit entrance of the palace. Ryan stepped down easily, aware of the figure he cut in the black, gold-embroidered *vaquero*'s garb he wore. Mason, his new ramrod, came up beside him. 'How many of us go in with you?'

Ryan shook his head. It was attention he wanted tonight more than protection. 'None of you. Keep them out of trouble here. No fighting. We'll ride back tonight, after the ball. They can get drunk in Lanyard tomorrow.'

He went up the great, stone steps, his Mexican-silver spurs a-jingle, and paused on the landing. Men and women made way for him, but he did not notice. He came into the foyer, and behind him the great bonfire in the plaza began to roar and red flames licked upward hungrily. The crowd roared their approval of the excitement. Ryan entered the grand ballroom and stopped at the entrance, aware that every head in the room swivelled towards him. He was a power in the land they could not ignore; he read envy and dislike and real hatred in their faces, and it pleased him. He came down the steps into the big room, walking with the born horseman's natural grace, and a way was cleared for him as people drew to one side to stare after his arrogant figure. On the flag-draped dais at the far end of the magnificent room, he saw the red-sashed shape of Governor Lew Walton and beside him stocky, black-bearded General Ulysses S. Grant. Ryan's eyes were bright and fixed to the governor's face as he walked slowly forward.

Outside, Billy Bascom had gained the rear of the *palacio.* It was dark and quiet, the gay noise of the crowd muted. There was a growing red glare in the sky from the burning bonfire, and Billy knew he must hurry. He edged behind an evergreen, ducked beneath an open, lighted window, darting a quick look inside. There was a hall beyond, lighted but empty, and in an instant his lithe figure swung up and over the windowsill, and he cat-footed it across carpeting to the dark recess of back stairs. He went up them at a run, breathing evenly. He felt no excitement, only a cold steady intent.

The upper hall ended at a balcony that overlooked the grand ballroom, and people lined the great balustrade, staring down excitedly. From this end of the balcony, between the gathered watchers, Billy could see the dais, and the black-clad man who slowly approached it. His own back stiffened, and his mouth thinned to a hard, cruel line. Then he whirled, ran the length of the balcony, his feet silent on the carpeting, and none of the intent onlookers noticed him. He gained the far end, darted through the velvet hangings that covered a stairway that descended to one side of the platform. There he paused, breathing hard, and thinking fast. Slowly, his crooked smile twisted his lips. A lamp burned at the head of the stairs, and he lifted it from its brackets, blew it out, and returned to the heavy draperies. He unscrewed the fuel cap, dumped the kerosene down the long, velvet curtains. It soaked in, spread idly, making a dark stain. He held the lamp in his right hand, dug out a match with his left, struck it across a mahogany panel of the wall, laid the yellow flame against the oil-soaked cloth. It caught with a muffled report, then ugly flames billowed out, enveloping the drapes. Instantly, Billy was away, taking the steps down four at a time, trailing the upturned lamp in his hand. He reached the bottom, another match flared, and the heavy carpet thundered into fire that raced upward. Thick smoke clogged the narrow stairway, and he knew it would burst across the balcony, fill the great dome of the ballroom.

The mirror-walled ballroom was hushed as Jason Ryan approached the governor's dais. The silence was a thickness in the air against which his spurs jangled imperiously. He reached the bottom of the platform, looked up arrogantly – then froze as a woman's terrified scream rang out. It was followed by a thunderous explosion that shook the walls, and made the crystal chandeliers sway crazily. The sound of breaking glass was instantaneous, and in the vacuum of sound that followed the dynamite's roar, smoke billowed crazily down from the high, arched dome, dimming the lamplight.

From beyond the palace, screams and yells and uproar shook the thick walls. A man yelled hoarsely: 'Mother of God, it's the end of the world!' Then others cried out, 'Fire!' Harsh, red light flared, making the bright lamps seem to pale. For an instant the crowded ballroom remained still, caught by the pressure of shocked panic – and then a man broke and ran for the doorway. Instantly there was a crazed, fighting surge toward the exits, and Lew Walton shouted in vain to restore order. Then guards moved hurriedly forward, and Walton and the bearded Grant were ushered away.

At the base of the dais, Jason Ryan stood still. His tall, hard figure spun about, unhurriedly, and the movement stopped.

'Now, Jason,' said Billy Bascom, his hard, flat voice lifting above the tumult of fear-crazed people and the fierce crackle of flames. There was no one near them; this entire end of the blazing ballroom was empty; only the smoke blurred images were reflected in the mirrored panels of the walls.

Billy moved slowly forward, and behind him flames licked up the velvet hangings, began to blacken the walls. A tapestry caught with a rifle-like report, and yellow fire exploded outward. Now it ends, Billy thought, and strangely there was no satisfaction in it, only the same cold determination. The shining hate deepened in his eyes, and his smile was gone. The game was played out, and it had lasted too long, and the fun was gone from it.

Ryan's rock of a face didn't change, but he knew there was no appeal, no chance, and no escape. This slight, almost frail figure of a boy was Death, certain and inevitable. God Almighty, has all I have done gone for nothing but this? The bitter thought tore at him. A man could build as high as the sky, destroying every man who got in his way – and one kill-crazy kid could bring him tumbling down. And, as his crimes would be forgotten so would his greatness. Everything he had built would fall and smash, and the little pieces would remind no one of what once they had represented – a man's whole life. The taste of ashes was bitter, and the stone-like strength of Ryan's face crumbled, suddenly and completely, and two tears rolled down his cheeks.

'Draw, goddamn you!' Billy yelled viciously. He saw the weakness that gripped Ryan, made his legs tremble. In the last, terrible instant of his life, Jason Ryan was humbled, his pride destroyed, and it revolted Billy as had nothing else before.

The bigger man read this in Billy's eyes, and it jarred something inside him. Slowly he straightened – and then with a movement that was incredibly swift like a flash of lightning, the black-clad figure bent to one side, and his heavy revolver was in hand.

Even as it came level, Billy's gun bucked against his hand, and he saw Ryan slammed back, off-balance, and his answering shot smashed the mirror behind the kid. Ryan went down to hands and knees, like an injured, resting fighter; then, mortally injured, his will more than his strength, he came erect. He fought to bring his Colt up, the effort beading his face with sweat. Then Billy's second shot crescendoed, hurled Ryan about as if struck by the weight of a running horse, and his revolver spun from his nerveless grasp. For an instant Ryan held there, staring into the eyes of his killer, and then he turned to walk away, his back straight, his arrogance once more in place. He took one step – two – then staggered and fell into a blazing tapestry, his crooked fingers pulling it down with him as he went.

For one long instant Billy stood there, staring down at his fallen enemy, at the fiery blanket that covered him, and then he turned and backed away. Smoke filled the great ballroom, and the shouted cries still echoed, but purposefully now, as men fought down panic and organized to fight the fire. Men cursed and shouted orders that no one obeyed, and in the confusion, the slim youth moved swiftly and was gone.

Little Jaime Rodriguez hurried through the night toward his home, and the streets of Lanyard were very dark and Jaime whistled, although he was truly not afraid. The good Padre Xavier had spoken all too well of the powers of evil that thronged the darkness, and it was an awareness of this that hustled Jaime's bare brown feet through the dust. He came abreast of an alleyway, and then halted, his heart pounding fiercely in his thin breast as a soft call reached him.

'*Muchacho*!' came the voice from the darkness. 'Do you want earn a peso?'

Jaime hesitated, torn between good sense and spiritual fear, and as is usually the case, fear lost out. '*Si*!' he answered.

'Then go to Sheriff Burnett – tell him the one he seeks is at the Maxton House tonight – and tell him the information is from Conchita Noriega – do not forget!'

A silver coin glinted dully in the meagre light, and landed at his feet. Jaime bent, picked it up, tested it between his teeth, then grinned. '*Si, Señorita*!' he promised, then stopped, puzzled. He sensed he was alone; the presence in the shadows was gone. And the voice – suddenly he realized it had not been that of a woman. Jaime felt his hackles rise, and his superstitious fears returned, sending him running as fast as his thin, brown legs could carry him. But the peso was in his pocket, and a bargain is a bargain – even with a demon, God forbid! He ran toward the sheriff's office.

Pete Burnett rode at the head of the silent, intent group of men. The night was warm and still, and the ride had been hard, yet Burnett was not tired. He held all thought to a minimum, covering just each moment as it passed, and not thinking ahead at all.

The deputy riding beside him asked, 'You figger this another wild-goose chase, Sheriff?'

'Anybody can guess,' Burnett replied.

The deputy grunted. 'Sure. But if Billy's really there, Conchita Noriega's goin' to be the richest damned half-breed in New Mexico. I keep wonderin' what she'll do with twenty thousand bucks – probably go to hell in a hurry, but at least she'll be travellin' in style.'

'Maybe that's what is important,' Burnett answered. The deputy glanced toward him, then lapsed into silence.

The yellow lights of the Maxton House gleamed through the night, and Pete Burnett drew up, his men halting behind him. 'Ride in slow, one at a time. Cover the yard and the road. He may be anywhere – or not here at all. If you see him, shoot. He won't hesitate to, and if you do, you're dead. I'll ride in first. Cover me.'

It was nearing dawn. The night was warm, and the new day would be hot. The promise was in the still air, in the humid pressure about them. Burnett urged his horse on, rode into the littered yard, and reined in. He dismounted, looping the reins over a hitch rail. He walked quietly over gravel to the sagging, broken porch, eased his weight up cautiously, and drew his gun. The screen door was ajar, and he pulled it open, stepped into the hall. Colonel Maxton had been failing rapidly, and his poster bed had been brought down to his study. It was there that Burnett made his way. He paused at the doorway. In the feeble light of a flickering candle set on a stand beside the bed, he saw the Colonel's pale figure and face.

Ben Maxton's eyes opened slowly. Recognition came into them, and his wasted, skeletal face smiled. 'Welcome, Pete,' he said, softly. 'Come in and sit a spell.'

Burnett crossed to the bed, every nerve ajangle. He sat gingerly on the edge of a straight back chair beside the bed. 'Howdy, Colonel,' he answered, gently. 'You had any company tonight?'

The faded blue eyes closed wearily. 'Tonight? I'm not sure, Pete. I'm tired. A man has no right to live so long.' His voice drifted away, and he began to breathe heavily, his mouth dropping open.

The noise of crickets in the fields was loud. The old house groaned, much as its dying master did in his sleep. Burnett sat on the edge of the chair, eyes wary, every sense alert, his gun in his hand. Then he stiffened. Outside, on the porch, he heard a soft step, and then a man's low '¿Quién es?'

The screen door squeaked, and steps came down the hall. Burnett came off the chair and went down to one knee, his revolver up, levelled. A stronger light came through the doorway, spilling shadows into the room. A slender form, holding a candle, stepped in.

'Colonel, who's here? Who are those men outside?' A revolver was in the slim man's hand, and his body was tensed like that of a jumping cat.

Burnett said, sadly, 'Billy, it's Pete.'

Holding the candle high, the youth whirled, bringing up the

gun. Burnett's hand moved in reflex action, and his own revolver spoke first; two sharp, violent crashes of sound. The thin figure jerked erect, then dropped silently to the floor. The candle fell, but did not go out, and Burnett came forward to pick it up. In the soft, flickering light, he saw Billy's face, gentle and smiling, and dead.

Then feet crashed and pounded, and the Colonel was calling out, and Burnett said, quietly, 'It's all right. It's all over.'

For a long time he stood there, remembering the good days, the young laughter. And then he murmured, softly, '*Vaya con Dios*, Billy,' and went outside.